THE
WILD WEST

Stories From Westside Wilmington

JUAN CARLOS DIAZ

Library of Congress Control Number: 2024918966

Paperback ISBN: 978-1-965092-43-9
Hardcover ISBN: 978-1-965092-44-6

Main category— Literature & Fiction Mystery, Thriller & Suspense › Crime
Other category— Short Stories & Anthologies › Short Stories › Action & Adventure › Men's Adventure

Published by: AR PRESS
Roger L. Brooks, Publisher
roger@americanrealpublishing.com
americanrealpublishing.com

TABLE OF CONTENTS

SAMMY POPPED HIS CHERRY

SEPTEMBER 8, 1990

WALKING DOWN BROOM STREET, I LET THE DARKNESS that encased me loosen its grip and dissolve into the night. I had just made my way past Palasky Elementary School when the memory of what I did stabbed my brain. My victim's screams, punctuating the stinging feeling in my soul, traveled down to the pit of my stomach. Bile rose from the back of my throat and landed on some potted plants in front of a house. I watched as the bile clung, white and ropey, from my chin, reminding me that I was still a novice when it came to killing another human being. True, I'd killed my girl's pops that spring, but that was different. That was a crime of passion. That piece of shit was hurting the woman I loved. I had to protect her, even if it cost me my life. But this hitman shit that Zepedas was having me do was way more than I could handle. I had to kill niggas that I didn't know, that never did any harm to me or mine. Those cats had wives, parents, and kids. At the time, it was really fucking me up that I had become Zepedas's personal Grim Reaper, but I had no choice. It was either them or me.

"Nigga, you need to learn how to compartmentalize," said Ace. I could tell he was trying to prepare me for my first contract killing.

"What the fuck you mean, *compartmentalize?*" I asked just as Ace blocked one of my kicks to his side, his gray Gold's Gym tank top soaked dark with sweat and clinging to his body.

Ace grew annoyed as weariness began to set upon his body like an invisible cloak. Seeing this as my opening for an attack, I quickly let loose with a barrage of jabs, breaking his guard. Once Ace's defenses were down, I came at him with two rapid rabbit punches to the jaw, stunning him. That gave me a wide opening to deliver a roundhouse kick to his face, dropping him like a sack of potatoes.

Lying flat on his back, Ace's chest heaved as he gulped for air. Seeing that victory was obtained from our little sparring session, I walked over to where he lay on the mat and gloated, "Maybe you should compartmentalize this beat down I just gave you, nigga." Suddenly, the training mat was swept from under me and the wind snatched from my lungs. I fell harshly on my back, head bouncing off the mat like a dribbled basketball.

With stars dancing in front of my eyes, I shook my head and saw Ace standing above me.

"That was a rookie mistake, dumbass. Never go up to your opponent after defeating him and gloat. You will leave an opening for a fatal blow. For example, I just used my leg to trip you. If I was another nigga, I would have shot you dead those few seconds that I had you on the ground. Your dumbass needs to learn how to control your emotions. This is part of the compartmentalization," Ace said smugly. Suddenly, his face morphed into the face of the nigga that I just killed at Camby Pool. disintegrating the memory of us sparring. No longer was I lying on the basement floor of our house staring up at him. Instead, I was back on the edge of Camby Pool, staring into the face of my victim before I executed him.

A faint glow of light emanated from the pool, giving the water a bluish glow that reminded me of radioactive waste. *Ha, they probably put those lights in there after they found Ace and his crew fucking a bunch of chicks in their pool last summer,* I thought, grinning. The smile quickly faded as my reason for being at Camby came back into focus. The darkness gripped me tighter, muting what remained of my conscience and transporting me back a week ago when I was sitting in front of Zepedas's desk, hearing him rant about one fuck up after another.

"What the fuck, man? If it isn't one fuck up, it's another," growled Zepedas, the extra skin on his meaty jowls swaying back and forth like pendulums. "This little piece of shit named Juni Reyes is diluting my cocaine. Word on the street is that he's mixing the coke with baby powder. Fuck, according to my man Cracky Johnson, he can't even get a buzz off it, which is driving away my usual customers."

To be honest, I had no idea what Juni's screw-up had to do with me, but I was loyal to Zepedas to a fault. Anything he needed done I did without question. It was as though I lived by that moral code since birth. I couldn't just disobey the man that put food on my table.

A brisk autumn wind suddenly pulled me out of my thoughts, planting me firmly on the sidewalk of Broom Street. To my surprise and disappointment, I was standing near the potted plants I vomited in. Maybe Ace was right, I really did need to learn how to compartmentalize.

"Nigga, we're soldiers. We can't be in our emotions every time a job needs to get done," Ace's voice echoed in my mind, ricochetting like a stray bullet. I made it to the end of the block where a phone booth stood like a lone sentry guarding against the demons of the night. The faint orange light of a streetlamp shone inside. As if the glow was an invitation, I quickly made my way inside the booth. A dome light overhead snapped on as I pulled back its door, hopped in, and closed it behind me. I fed the coin slot a quarter and put the receiver up to my ear. The howling wind shook the booth vigorously, as if it were a ghost desperately trying to get in and abscond with my corrupted soul.

With a trembling finger, I punched in the number to one of Zepedas's henchmen. I heard the shrill ringing on the other end, strangely reminding me of a sick baby's croupy cough. It was abruptly cut off by a gruff and burly, "Hello."

"Nigga, you ain't supposed to say hello," I said angrily.

"Oh, you calling about the Camby's hit? Is it done?"

Shaking my head in disgust, I said, "What do you think, dumbass!"

Before the guy could answer, I hung up the receiver and quickly exited the phone booth, desperately trying to leave the stupidity that seemed to have mired the booth.

"Jesus, all that asshole had to do was answer the phone and listen to me say that the hit was done," I said aloud with a deep sigh, letting out my frustration. *Now, if the fucking cops had that phone booth tapped, they would have one leg up in the investigation when they found Juni's body floating in the pool,* I thought, letting my imagination run wild. I needed to calm down before I vomited all over myself. I knew just who could help me out with that. A smile broke through my worries as the image of my love came to mind. I felt my stomach unclench and my anxiety loosen its grip on my chest. Suddenly, I was a regular dude. It was like I never even put two shots in a kid and threw his corpse in a public pool. Yup, the thought of my Sheila cleansed my soul of all the dirt and grime. She was my heavenly blindness. I could do no wrong by her.

With these thoughts circling my mind like hummingbirds on a spring day, I quickly reentered the phone booth. Feeding the phone another quarter, I dialed Sheila's number. Phone tap be damned. As her phone rang on the other end, I wondered what time it was, hoping she was still awake. She picked up on the fifth ring.

"Hello," she said. Her voice was thick with sleep, making me regret calling her and question whether I should be calling her so late.

"Did I wake you, babe?" I asked, already knowing the answer.

"Nigga, what do you think?" she asked with sarcasm-drenched grogginess.

That's my girl, I thought, stifling a laugh.

"Hey, Mamma Yadi ain't home, is she?" As soon as the question left my mouth, I suddenly became aware of how eager those words sounded. I felt the heat of embarrassment spread across my face. Suddenly, the phone booth I stood in felt like a closed casket cutting off my breath. *Damn, she probably thinks I'm desperate for some pussy now,* I thought nervously, looking down at my Adidas.

"Damn, dude, you really wanna see me right now, huh?" Sheila let out a come-hither laugh, as if saying, *come here and tear off these panties, Papi.*

"So, I take it from your little sexy giggle that she's not home," I said in a sly tone as my manhood stiffened.

"Nah, she had to work the late shift at St. Francis. You know how lazy motherfuckers be down in the laundry section of that hospital. Shit, someone's always calling out sick," Sheila said annoyingly, but I could tell that talking to me was keeping her anger at bay.

Believe me, I could totally understand Sheila's annoyance with Mamma Yadi filling in for someone at the hospital. The woman was just months away from retirement due to sciatica and a bad case of osteoporosis, which had her almost hunched over. Seeing Mamma Yadi like that would break my heart. She practically raised us for God's sake. For those who didn't have a mother on the Westside, Mamma Yadi was it. She didn't care what race you were or where you came from. She was always there with a home-cooked Puerto Rican meal, a place to stay, and a shoulder to cry on. Hell, she even gave Sheila a permanent home after I smashed Sheila's father's head in with a sledgehammer after I discovered that he had sexually abused her. Man, Mamma Yadi was a life saver for Sheila. It's a damn shame that she couldn't have kids of her own, because she would have been a great mother.

"Hello? Sammy, you still there?" Sheila asked on the other end of the receiver, bringing me back to the cramped confines of the phone booth.

"Uh, yeah," I said sheepishly. Suddenly, a warm wave of embarrassment blanketed my face, causing me to break out into a nervous sweat. *Oh God, what if she thinks I'm a loser?* I thought. Oddly enough, the hit I had just done diminished its grip on my anxiety, leaving me alone with my teenage awkwardness.

"Ah, you have your head in the clouds again. That's so typical of you," said Sheila, giggling.

"Oh, I see that you have jokes," I said, my anxiety floating away. It was as though I had never committed a murder prior to that conversation. That's how free Sheila made me feel. The only person in my life to make me feel like I was worth a damn. But the question that was eating away the fabric of my mind was this: *What would she think if she knew that I just killed a man, let alone if said man was the boyfriend of Chardey, Sheila's homegirl?* Man, if Sheila knew that she would leave my ass with the quickness. Shit, she'd probably come out her damn self, knowing how close they were. The bond between the two girls was thicker than blood. As a matter of fact, Sheila and I weren't almost a thing, thanks to my man Ace dogging Chardey. That shit had me in the doghouse with Sheila for months. I wasn't getting any play whatsoever. It was through the grace of God, however, that Sheila was able to look past my association with Ace and see the real me. This shit with Juni, though, opened up a fresh new hell.

"Ay yo, I'll be at your crib in a few," I said, trying to push back all of those thoughts about Juni.

"I'll be here with soaking wet panties, nigga. You better get your ass over here before I finish the job I want you to do myself," said Sheila, lacing her comment in the smooth fabric of a flirtatious giggle.

"Girl, you wild," I said with a snicker. "I'll be there in a few."

I hung up the phone as a force of excitement swept over my body, encompassing every fiber of my being. Suddenly, a sense of abandon took over my brain and I gave three swift kicks to the phone, causing it to bleed out an avalanche of coins. Bending down to scoop up a handful, I said to myself, "Damn, I need to calm the fuck down. All of this excitement over pussy." My words seemed to bounce off the walls of the phonebooth. Man, I could hear Ace's voice echo throughout my mind. *Nigga, don't let pussy rule you. Shit, pussy will kill you faster than a bullet.*

"Shut the fuck up, Ace," I said aloud as I exited the booth. The cool damp autumn wind caressed my face, as if trying to gain access to mind. Its all-seeing eyes had borne witness to my crime, not wanting to let a drop of happiness enter my heart. Taking two steps away from the phone booth, the corpses of little brown leaves had begun to swirl at my feet, making me feel like my body had stepped into a small tornado.

Suddenly, the cool autumn wind grew harsher in its force, making it seem like it was coming from the mouth of an invisible beast. I could feel the wind getting colder and colder, as it touched my eyelids, seeping into my eye sockets to gain entry to my brain. As crazy as it may sound, it was as though the wind was saying, *no, motherfuckers, you need to see the pain that you have caused.* And with that, my thoughts were transported to Juni's hit. No longer was I walking on a Broom Street sidewalk. My Adidas clad feet were firmly planted on the white tiles around Camby Pool. It was then that I realized the darkness was once again forcing me to relive the hit on Juni that happened less than an hour ago.

"Yo, what's good, my nigga!" exclaimed Juni.

His voice hit my ears before I physically saw him, scaring the shit out of me. Looking up, I saw Juni walking in my direction from across the street. Saint Elizabeth's Church loomed behind him, as if it was a golem birthed from monsters of fine masonry. *Look out now, the kid has a Gundam,* I thought, stifling a laugh.

I watched him make his way from across the street with his hands deep in his jeans pockets, hunched over with a baggy red and blue Tommy Hilfiger jacket. The strong wind was puffing the sleeves up, making Juni's wiry frame look muscular. His faded blue jeans sagged from his hips, exposing the plaid waistband of his Hanes boxers. His Timberland shoes made Juni's attire complete, setting off the curly black locks that bounced atop his head as he moved.

"What's up, dude?" yelled Juni as he made his way toward me.

"What up, man?" I said, giving him a dap hug.

"Ay yo, I didn't know you was my new connect. That's good shit, though. You moving up in the world, huh? From corner boy to connect. How the hell did you pull that off?" Juni asked, not bothering to conceal his envy. If Juni had an ounce of intelligence, he would know that it was virtually impossible for a mere corner boy to be an actual connector. But then again, if Juni was smart, he wouldn't have stepped on his drugs so much, causing a hit to be put on him.

Pulling away from our embrace, I quickly pulled out the .38 pistol that I had hidden in my jeans pocket and shot Juni point blank in the chest. The bullet was starting to form a grotesque scarlet on the front of his jacket. Feeling my stomach begin to tie itself in knots, my eyes moved to Juni's face, which had the saddest and most haunting expression I had ever seen in my life. That expression was a mixture of betrayal and shock. It seemed to say, *why did you have to do me like that, fam?* As if passing that final thought to me took his last ounce of strength, Juni fell like a marionette whose puppet master had discarded its strings.

With my .38 still in hand, I walked over to Juni's lifeless body and put a slug in the middle of his forehead, but not before looking into his eyes. Those eyes that seemed to hold so much of our friendship in them. Crystalized in his irises were our memories. The time we took Charde and Sheila to the Puerto Rican Day Parade and acted like fools, stealing as much food as we could from the vendors that walked up and down the street. Or the time we first played Atari at my crib, Juni showing me how to play *Crystal Castles.* Damn, he was like a brother to me, and I killed him.

Seized with a sudden primal urge to run, I was struck with the childish superstition that Juni's ghost was going to grab me and pull me down to hell as soon as I turned my back. So, as I left the scene, I backed away slowly from the corpse. My eyes were glued to it as if waiting for it to come alive like a zombie from a George Romero film. Of course, logic soon swept over me, which gave me the courage to turn my back and gain strength in my legs to run out of Camby's and make my way to Broom Street, where I ended up vomiting in someone's flowerpot.

In that moment, I felt that memory loosen its grip on me. Suddenly I was standing on the corner of West Fourth Street, which faced the Saint Paul Church rectory. I could feel a wave of relief wash over me as I realized that I was two doors down from Sheila's. However, I had no idea how I arrived there. It was as if my body functioned on autopilot while my conscience forced me to face the atrocity I had committed. Shaking away the residue that was left behind from the cobwebs of my thoughts, I dug my hands into my jeans pockets and let the skin between my fingers linger on the coolness of the coins that filled them. This slight motion was surprisingly soothing to me, killing whatever anxiety I had left.

Like almost everyone who lived in Westside Wilmington, Sheila and Mamma Yadi lived in a row home, attached to other homes, which reminded me of giant Siamese twins joined at the hip until death. Their house was part of a set of homes that used to be a Catholic school in the early 1900s, which were later turned into homes in the mid-1960s. However, nothing that resembled a school was left except for the old fire escapes that led from the street to the second floor. I gained access to them via a chain link gate that opened onto a small backyard, which also housed a small garden.

Noticing that the gate was unlocked, I stepped inside and crept up the fire escape, blending into the shadows. *Damn, I do one hit, and suddenly I'm 007 blending into shadows and shit.* This thought ran through my mind as though trying to shine a light on the darkness of the atrocity that I had committed. Instead of diminishing its grotesqueness, the light only increased it, showing me how my soul was beginning to rot. Moving further ahead, my heart started to pound incessantly as the pool of light from Sheila's bedroom shone brightly on the cool black surface of the rusted fire escape, pulling me toward her window like a tractor beam.

Little bits of the baseline of Cynthia and Johnny O's "Dream Boy/Dream Girl" seeped out through the closed window. The very baseline itself was making my heart beat with the rhythm, proving to me that I wasn't a monster. Giving a silent thank you to God—yeah, despite the fact that I just killed someone, I still believe there's a God we have to answer to—I positioned myself in front of her bedroom and rapped on the windowpane lightly. The walls of Sheila's bedroom radiated a soft glow of baby pink, casting everything in deep shadows. From the corner of my eye, I became aware that a silhouette was beginning to form on the section of carpet that led to the bedroom door. My heart pounded madly, like a crazed ape banging on the bars of its cage, for I knew that my beloved was coming to greet me.

Suddenly, Sheila was on the other side of the window with a huge smile plastered on her face, and a come-hither look that made her eyes dance with lust. Her chestnut hair cascaded down her back, a waterfall reflecting her Taino ancestry. Her eyes were the green of velvety moss, giving her an ethereal look that no other girl her age possessed. It was as though Sheila's soul was housed within them, viewing the world from its throne.

"Damn nigga, you coming in or not?" asked Sheila, her voice dragging me out of my reverie.

"My bad, Ma," I said, with a big cheesy grin on my face. She rolled her eyes playfully and opened her window to let me in. As I ducked my head to enter her bedroom, a cold wind blew across the back of my neck. It felt like the cold hand of Death, reminding me of the life I took no more than thirty minutes ago. With my Adidas firmly planted on the carpet, I wasted no time in checking out the body of my beautiful Borinquen queen. The first thing my eyes landed on was the small tank top she had on, hugging the suppleness of her

C-cup breasts, making my manhood stiffen to its full mass. My eyes began to roam over the curved valleys of her hips and slowly moved down her slightly exposed navel to a pair of white cotton panties, which complemented her mocha skin.

As if hearing my lust calling her, Sheila stepped closer to me and planted her lips on mine, tasting of bubble gum lip gloss.

"What's up with your hoodie, babe? It has these reddish-brown speckles all over it," she said with a mixture of fear and disgust. Looking down at my cream Adidas hoodie, I noticed the speckles that she was talking about. Until that moment, I had no idea that Juni's blood had gotten all over me. I could hear Ace now. *"You dumbass, how the hell could you not know that blood would get on you after you shoot a nigga?"*

"What the hell did you do, Sam?"

That was the question that broke me. Its tone of fear and disgust forged with what seemed to be my true reflection. The reflection of a monster. To make matters worse, I knew that was how Sheila saw me in her heart. I couldn't bear the thought of her seeing me like that. To say that I wanted to die was an understatement. I could feel my soul clawing at my insides, trying desperately to break free from the prison that was my body. Unfortunately, the only thing that my soul could manage as an escape was to retreat deep into my tear ducts and glide down my cheeks. *What a futile attempt to escape,* I thought, letting huge sobs out like heavy boulders. I suddenly found myself sitting on the edge of Sheila's bed, hunched over with my hands covering my face. The heat of embarrassment stung my cheeks.

"I don't want to be a monster, Sheila. Please, you gotta believe me, babe. I was just following the orders that were given to me." The litany oozing out of my mouth was a garbled mixture of groans, moans, and sobs. It was a miracle she could understand me at all. Jesus, I felt like such a pussy at that moment, but when I looked up, Sheila's facial expression was one of concern and pain. It was as though she was witnessing something die inside of me before her very eyes. That was when she seemed to let go of some of her apprehension and sat beside me on her bed, taking me in her arms and rocking me gently back and forth.

"It's okay, babe, you're safe here with me. You can tell me what happened. I won't judge you, I swear to God. Anyway, I would be a hypocrite to judge the man who killed my step-dad to save me." Sheila's proclamation washed over me like a soothing warm balm. I looked into her eyes and saw that she was just as broken as me. That's when I decided to tell her everything about Juni's murder.

Her face was as impassive as stone as she listened to my words, soaking it all in. When I finished, Sheila cleared her throat and said, "It wasn't your fault. You had a job to do and you did it. If you hadn't completed the hit, it would have been your ass, babe. Do you think Juni would've had pity on you if the roles were reversed? I know you guys were cool, but you had a job to do. As cruel as this may sound, Juni was a rat that needed to be exterminated. Rumor has it, he was an informant for the cops. Not to mention that he was stepping on the coke way too much. So much so, I would say that Juni's coke was practically baby powder."

Sheila's words seeped into my thoughts as she sat beside me holding my hand. Looking into her eyes, I finally saw how broken she was. It was as though I was in a time warp. Suddenly, I saw Sheila as a five-year-old standing in front of her mother's corpse as it hung from a rope tied around her neck. The corpse swayed to and fro as a slight breeze passed through an open window. Next, I bore witness to another horrific scene. In this particular one, I saw an eight-year-old

Sheila, her screams echoing throughout the room as her step-dad lay on her, pounding away on her little womanhood until he came.

I'm so glad I killed that bastard when I did.

"Are you listening to me?" Sheila asked, her words dragging me out of the time warp that I was in. I looked at her, confused. She rolled her eyes at me.

"Nigga, your ass is always daydreaming. It doesn't matter what situation you're in, you always find time to. Anyway, I was asking how much is your boss paying you for the Juni hit?"

"Fifteen hundred," I blurted without a thought.

"What the fuck! Nigga...you got played. A hit like that should get you at least two mil, easy." Sheila said, with a scrunched-up face of disgust.

"You think Zepedas is taking advantage of me?" I asked, knowing the answer to that question.

"Of course he is, Sammy. He sees that you're young and inexperienced. That alone makes him feel like he can control you every which way he sees fit. Face it, Sam, you're Zepedas's pawn," Sheila said matter-of-factly, making me feel uncomfortable. That's when I decided to change the topic.

"Man, Chardey is gonna be a mess when she finds out," I said sadly.

"Nah, she'll get over it," Sheila said nonchalantly. "Besides, she knew that the bastard was cheating on her with Yadira, anyway. I don't think she'll shed a tear for that nigga."

"Wait, you mean to tell me that Juni was fucking Yadira from fifth period science class?" I said, giggling in surprise. "Man, that's one ugly bitch. She looks like a damn Muppet Baby."

Sheila laughed so hard at this that she fell off the bed, grabbing her belly. I loved her laugh so much. The way it seemed to coat every wall of her bedroom with a teenaged innocence. Suddenly, the sound of laughter ceased.

Clearing her throat, Sheila said, "Hold up, you said that Juni was your first kill, but that ain't true. You killed my stepdad, remember?"

As if to keep the good vibes going, I said, "That I did. However, killing your stepdad was a pleasure for me. The motherfucker was hurting you. I had to defend you even if it meant my life. With Juni, though, he was my first paid hit. He was my homie. I had love for the dude, you know?"

"I know what you mean, Papi. I don't know if I could kill Chardey if I had to," said Sheila, laying her head on my shoulder. We let the silence linger heavily upon us, like a thick winter blanket that absorbed the innocence leaking out of our being.

Meanwhile, the city was weeping with the sound of police sirens, mourning the loss of another young soul.

CRACKY JOHNSON'S BIG SCORE

"Yo, this shit's for the birds, man," Keon said to no one in particular.

Watching his breath collide with the mid-January air, he thought he would rather be anywhere in the world than out there on the corner of Lancaster and Harrison, selling crack to fiends like a discombobulated assembly line. Keon hated that shit with a passion. Every time a crack fiend came up to him to request how many vials they wanted, they stunk of death and excrement. To Keon, these people were the living dead, lost to the world. They were just husks that housed tortured souls, waiting for God to call them home. Sure, he felt terrible providing these fiends their high, but if they weren't getting it from him and his boys, they would get it from someone else. Plus, Keon felt that he needed to help his mom out with the bills that were piling up. He wasn't trying to be noble, but he'd be damned if he let his mom be thrown out on the street: a woman who held down two jobs. She was a lunch lady at H.B. DuPont Middle School during the day, and a cleaning lady at the Day's Inn on Route 13 by night. He hated seeing break her back like that. It broke Keon's heart. Not to mention he felt like shit lying to her about where his money came from. In her mind, he was working as a stock boy at a bodega on Fourth Street, commonly known as Papi's.

To make himself feel less guilty about where his money came from, Keon often reminded himself that he *indeed* was on the bodega's payroll, just not in the conventional way. He sold drugs from Papi's, and in return, he would make Keon look like a legitimate worker, complete with W2 forms and all. He was just glad that his mother was antisocial and lived out in the boondocks. That way she never had to roll past his corner on the way to work or listen to gossip about him being on the streets. Or so his teenage mind worked out to make himself feel better.

"Hey young blood, what's good wit' ya?" A gravelly voice pulled Keon out of his thoughts, dragging his nerves over the coarseness of its sound.

"What the fuck do you want, Cracky?" said Keon, rolling his eyes at the addict in front of him.

"Come on, man. Ain't you ever heard of respecting your elders?" said Cracky, offended by Ken's tone.

"Look man, I ain't got time for your bullshit today, I'm serious." Keon eyed the addict from head to toe, letting his eyes glide up and down the man's six-foot frame. His torso donned a tattered football jersey with the name "McNabb" emblazoned on the back. The number five on the jets was in shredded little pieces, barely hanging onto the fabric, as if someone had rudely taken apart a jigsaw puzzle and left the pieces close to one another. Also, along the raggedy jersey's surface were splotches of what seemed to be dried blood or mud. The shirt was so old that it was difficult to determine. Moving his view down to Cracky's legs, Keon noticed the man sported camouflage pants that were ripped at both knees, giving the addict an aura of a homeless Vietnam vet. That particular image would sometimes haunt Keon, paralyzing him in fear because he knew that sooner or later, he'd have to look into the vortex of pain that were Cracky's eyes.

His face didn't do him any favors either. It was as though the flesh on his entire skull was holding on for dear life, making it seem that one false movement of the head would make the flesh on his entire life fall off like cheese from a slice of pizza with extra sauce. His facial features carried a road map of pain physically etched into his face, dried up riverbeds of time. Strangely enough, however, Cracky's eyes held a youthfulness that seemed eternal. It was as though the man's soul roamed the world for a million years before settling in his body. It was obvious to everyone living in Westside Wilmington that Cracky Johnson lived quite a life on the streets. Rumor had it, the guy had served in Vietnam as part of the first deployment of US Marines to land Da Nang in March of 1965. Once his troop came ashore, they were swallowed by a sweltering jungle, disorienting the entire troop. It caused them to forget all about their destination, which was a small fishing village south of the shore. Sadly, most of Cracky's troops were killed off one by one, leaving him to fend for himself.

For two weeks, he made his way through the labyrinth of the jungle, surviving on whatever animals he killed with his knife. Battered and bloodied and in the throes of delirium, Cracky managed to arrive at the troop's destination. It was there that he was taken prisoner, bound, and beaten within an inch of his life in a crater-sized hole dug six feet underground, making him feel like he was buried alive. Cracky could still feel the stinging of the lashes brought on by the leather straps his captors used to whip him with. Strangely enough, Keon could feel all of the pain stored in Cracky's soul every time he looked into his eyes. It was as though the man's tortured soul was encapsulated in the jewel of his iris for the world to see.

"You know the deal, homie. You better step the fuck off," said Keon, trying to mask the pity he felt for the man with bravado.

"What you mean *step off*, little nigga? How the fuck you gonna deny me my medicine when I got the money to pay for it?" Cracky said, with anger clawing its way out of his mouth.

"Man, you know damn well that Papi don't want us selling you no more," countered Keon.

"Aw hell, young blood, don't listen to that damn spic. That dude kinda retarded. Who in they right mind denies money?" Cracky said, disgusted.

"Look dude, I don't know the specifics, but all the corner boys working for Papi were told not to sell any drugs to you, not even aspirin." Keon said in a rehearsed tone.

"Look, you little shit. I put my time in with Papi for years. That motherfucker owes me," Cracky growled, stepping closer into Keon's space. Now almost touching nose to nose, Keon could smell Cracky's breath as it carried the stench of rotting teeth.

"Man, back the fuck up, nigga," said Keon, putting his hand on the butt of his 9mm pistol, ready to pull it out of the waistband of his boxers at moment's notice.

"You think I'm scared of you, young blood? I was a POW in Vietnam. Every day I was beaten within an inch of my life. So, you see, that little pistol you got hidden in your underwear won't put a scratch on me," said Cracky confidently.

"Shut the fuck up, nigga!" Without giving it any thought, Keon whipped his pistol and fired four consecutive shots to the chest. The force of the bullets piercing his chest rocked Cracky off his feet, causing his head to slam on the pavement. Dazed for a few seconds, Cracky shook his head and got back to his feet as if nothing happened.

"Fuck, that hurt like a bitch," he said groggily, trying to get the world to stop floating in front of his eyes. Placing one hand underneath his chin and the other at the base of his skull,

Cracky's neck made a satisfying crunch sound, establishing the world back on its axis.

The sound of gunfire put the entire block into a whirlwind of chaos. Men, women, and children were seeking cover, but that didn't mean anything to Cracky and Keon. The two men were in their own world of horror.

"What the fuck, I just shot four times at point blank range," said Keon, surprised that he didn't stutter out of fear.

Suddenly, Cracky was towering over Keon, casting a huge shadow over the teen. Closing whatever space was left between them, Cracky lowered his face, eye level with Keon and growled, "You tell that bitch-ass boss of yours I'm gonna get what he owes me."

Distracted by the stench of Cracky's tooth decay, mingling with the fear that pounded in his heart, Keon barely had time to notice the pocketknife that pierced his stomach three times in rapid succession.

"Yeah, who's the cocky one now, nigga?!" said Cracky, lacing his words with a triumphant cackle. Not thinking about the possibility of the cops pulling up on him, he stood there with a big smile plastered on his face, watching the kid's body slide down the brick wall and die. He slowly closed his eyes and let his head fall forward. It always mesmerized Cracky how the human soul left the body, its muscles stiffening, leaving it to resemble a marionette that had been abandoned by its puppet master.

"Well, I'll be damned, the little shit looks like a piece of art," said Cracky to himself, tilting his head like a dog staring at a piece of meat. He was knocked out of his thoughts when he felt a jarring sensation on the left side of his body. Suddenly, he was well aware of the world around him. People were running and screaming for their lives, desperately seeking shelter from the gunfire. Anxiety began to surge through his body, forcing him to move and think fast for fear of getting caught by the police. Cracky's eyes immediately zeroed in on Keon's coat pockets, which were bulging with vials of crack cocaine. Digging in the pockets of Keon's bubble coat, Cracky's came up with a fistful of small crack vials, causing a surge of jubilation to course through him. Not caring about how he looked at that moment, Cracky put the drugs and blade into his pockets, thanking God for the deep pockets of his pants.

With his newfound energy, Cracky made it to a secluded alley two blocks away from the murder he had just committed. Sitting down with his back against a rotted wooden fence, Cracky dug in his pockets once again and produced a crack pipe and a lighter. Opening up one of the vials, he poured the substance into the pipe as the flame ignited from the bottom of the pipe. As he heard the tiny crack crystals start to pop and simmer, he put his dry, cracked lips to the mouth of the pipe and began to inhale. Suddenly, all of Cracky's muscles started to loosen its grip on his being, relaxing and caressing the cramps of his cravings away. The man was at peace. That was when Cracky began to submerge him into a sea of his memories drowning out the present.

No longer was he in a secluded back alley smoking his crack pipe. Instead, Cracky found himself back in that godforsaken pit, naked with his hands and feet shackled, receiving multiple lashes from a leather whip that was controlled by his Vietnamese captor. The stench of Cracky's own excrement and urine assaulted his senses as the stinging of the lashes on his back rained agony down upon him. Large chunks of Cracky's flesh peeled off like strips of wallpaper. The pain had grown so intense that he found himself moving in and out of consciousness. It wasn't long before he found himself wishing for Death's merciful hand to be put upon his shoulder and free him, but his only solace was when the black sea of unconsciousness would swallow him whole.

Luck would shine upon Cracky, however. In one of his many bouts to not let the blackness consume him anymore, Cracky became aware that there was another person shackled in that pit with him. He noticed that the same captor that beat him was now going to town on another man with the same leather strap. The captor delivering blows was a scrawny-looking man, so skinny and emaciated that it was hard to believe that those hellish blows were coming from him. The man's bamboo hat barely fit atop his small head, seeming to almost swallow it. His clothes were so ill-fitting on his body that air would often seep into his pants and inflate them, like he was about to float away like a balloon.

As Cracky took notice of all this, he became aware that the other prisoner was a US soldier, judging from his camouflage pants and combat boots. The big toe of his left boot poked out of a large hole like an unruly child sticking out his tongue. The soldier's torso was bare, exposing a chest with thick black hair that matched the matted, coarse hair on his arms. The prisoner was ripped with muscles and had a six pack that would make the average man jealous. This gave off the indication that Cracky's fellow prisoner was athletic and could probably kick some ass. *If that's so, how the hell did he get caught by these skinny bastards?* These thoughts ran through Cracky's mind as he observed his fellow prisoner getting the living shit beat out of him. It wasn't like he felt sorry for the guy or anything, but he found it odd that despite the horrendous beating he was receiving, the man had a crazed grin on his face.

"That motherfucker has completely lost it," Cracky whispered to himself. He could feel a sudden fear creep into his heart, making him feel as if he was staring at the face of the devil himself. The fear was so overwhelming that Cracky closed his eyes as if to ward off the evil that emanated from the prisoner.

"Ha, give it to me, bastards! Give me my power, gook," the prisoner ranted as the captor's whip smacked against his flesh, peeling away strips of skin. Suddenly, the prisoner released a baritone rush of laughter, which ricocheted off the walls of the pit. The laughter encompassed the atmosphere, a demonic aura that even put the captor himself on edge. Noticing this, the prisoner lifted his low hanging head, smiling like a village idiot with spittle dripping down his chin. His full head of black curls outlined with the faint yellowish orange of the late afternoon sun, making him resemble a fallen angel.

"Thanks for giving back my power, brother," said the prisoner to the captor, as if they were old buddies looking for something that had been lost for decades in an old, dank basement. The captor's face suddenly became a portrait of confusion, as he realized that the prisoner was actually *enjoying* what was being done to him. Surging with a burst of energy, the prisoner broke free of his shackles, sending them flying like ninja stars and slicing open the captor's throat.

Watching this unfold before his eyes, Cracky couldn't help but feel extreme jubilation as he saw his captor bleed out before his eyes, looking as helpless as a deer caught in headlights. Cracky couldn't help but release a sound of childlike glee that had been buried inside him for decades. The sound was strange and foreign to him, but the thought was quickly swiped from his mind when he saw his fellow prisoner walking toward him nonchalantly, as though he was just stepping out for an evening stroll.

Without physically touching the shackles that bound his limbs, he freed Cracky. The shackles fell limply from his ankles and wrists with a simple wave of the man's hand, allowing him to weakly fall to his knees.

"What the fuck, man? Are you Jesus Christ or some shit?" Cracky let that question escape from his mouth with a mixture of fear and awe, allowing him to ask God to forgive him for his blasphemy.

"No, not even close, man. Hell, I'm more of an abomination," said the prisoner with a cocky smirk. Taking a good look at the man's face, Cracky quickly noticed that he had Latin features, most noticeably a smooth island tan that can only be given at birth. His cool, yet honey brown eyes suggested that that the soul inside of his body was dead, and his physical form was just waiting to rot away. Whatever Cracky was looking at he knew that it wasn't human, but he didn't care. The *thing* did save his life after all, and he was grateful for that.

"What's your name, boss?" asked the man as he helped Cracky to his feet.

"Ron Johnson," answered Cracky, feeling an immense weakness encompassing his entire body. Waves and waves of nausea began to assault Cracky, causing him to dry heave. Suddenly he was lying on the ground on his side, clutching his stomach.

"Easy, easy, I've got you." Kneeling down and placing his hands on Cracky's chest, the prisoner began to speak in a strange tongue, a dialect that had been abandoned by the world ages ago. A staggering pain gripped Cracky's heart, making him gasp in horror. With his eyes wide open, he became aware of what he was looking at. No longer was Cracky seeing a man. Before his eyes was a demon, one that Cracky knew deep in his heart that was expelled from heaven all the way to the depths of hell.

"Don't be afraid, Ron. You're dying and I'm here to save you. There is no fear in what I am about to give you. Rest now, Ron…become death with me."

As those final words penetrated and took shape in his mind, Cracky felt his body grow limp as his spirit started to climb out of his body, exiting through his mouth, leaving him in complete darkness.

When he came to, everything was a blur. Cracky's body screamed in pain. It was as though his entire body was one exposed nerve, being constantly stomped on by careless children. As his vision started to clear up, he noticed that he was in some sort of hospital unit. The sounds of doctors and nurses moving to and fro assaulted his senses. Closing his eyes to ward off the dizziness, all Cracky could see was that horrible demon in its godforsaken pit. The way it stood in the sun was almost regal in nature, its hair flowing long and silky in the light breeze. Its body white as the driven snow and rippling muscles from head to toe put to shame the average man. Marveling at what he was looking at, Cracky looked at the demon's face, which was a bloodred skull with burning flames in its eye sockets. Oddly enough, not an ounce of fear diluted his senses. The way he saw it was that the thing had saved his life, and he was grateful. But how could he remember all of this if he blacked out? Perhaps he was remembering a nightmare that he once had. Or maybe he was remembering a scene from a horror movie he saw as a kid. Whatever it was, Cracky was just grateful that he was no longer a prisoner in that damn pit.

"Well, you're welcome, Johnson. I aim to please."

"What the fuck?" mumbled Cracky, startled. Opening his eyes, he saw the Latin soldier from the pit standing at the foot of his hospital bed in a doctor's lab coat.

"I'm glad you're feeling better. For a while there it was touch and go, but it looks like you've made it out of the woods, which is extremely good news," said the doctor with a toothy grin, reminding Cracky of the old saying about the cat that stole the canary.

"Did you just read my mind?" Cracky asked, totally disregarding what the doctor had just told him.

"Why yes, I did," said the doctor moving to the head of the bed and whispering into Cracky's ear. "If you're also wondering, I'm the demon that helped you out of that dreadful pit." This somehow didn't faze Cracky. His face was impassive, not showing any emotion whatsoever. That impressed the demon.

Suddenly, Cracky hit the demon with a barrage of questions. "First of all, who or what the fuck are you? Second, why did you save me, and lastly, why did you bring me here?"

Those questions hung in the air as if waiting for the demon to throw a bread crumb, so that they could swoop down and gobble it up. "Okay, okay, take it easy, man. I'll answer all your questions," said the demon in between giggles. The demon grabbed a clipboard to make it seem like he was a doctor discussing a patient's condition.

"Motherfucker, why did you save me from that pit?" Cracky said, now almost in hysterics. Suddenly, he was feeling bold. There was no fear in him whatsoever. True, a demon was talking to him face-to-face, but as his grandmother had taught him, anything created by the devil was inferior.

"Well, well, look at you being all manly and accretive," said the demon mockingly as he closed the privacy curtain around their perimeter.

"Man, you really think I'm scared of you, huh? Shit, some demon you are. You all dressed up like a pretty boy Puerto Rican. What, is that how you get chicks to throw their panties at you?" Cracky let all this sarcasm spew from his soul, hoping to make a dent in the cocky demeanor of the demon, but to no avail. Seeing this, Cracky became relentless in his onslaught of insults.

"Oh, and another thing, you look really stupid in your demon form. Do you know who you look like? You look like that Captain America villain, Red Skull." That last statement seemed to slither out of Cracky's smile, like a snake emerging from its nest.

"Ha, you're a funny guy, Johnson," said the demon, a cool stare burrowing into his eyes. A sharp pain suddenly invaded Cracky's left breast, causing him to grab it. It was obvious to him that the demon was somehow crushing his heart with its mind. The pain was excruciating. He could barely breathe, let alone talk. While Cracky's eyes formed into slits of pain, he could see the demon grinning in its human form as it walked to the head of Cracky's hospital bed.

"Now listen, you little shit. I know you fear me right now, but you don't want to show it. I have peered into your soul and am well aware that you are scared shitless of me. As a matter of fact, I can literally hear your soul scream every time that you look at me. Now, look here. I play a huge role in your world. I'm what's known as a fallen angel, one of God's creations that followed Lucifer down to hell when he was expelled from heaven." The demon smiled as it observed fear flooding Cracky's widening eyes.

"That's right, Ron, show me your fear. Let me feed off it," said the demon, closing his eyes in what appeared to be ecstasy, as it sniffed the air. Suddenly Cracky felt the pain in his chest begin to dissipate and the death grip on his heart start to loosen. Drenched in sweat, he could feel a cool wave roll over his entire body, causing him to thank God out loud as he laid his head back on the sweaty pillow.

Not to be detected from what was being said, the demon kept on talking, noticing the relief on Cracky's face.

"You're welcome, motherfucker. I hope you know that I could kill with one swipe of my finger if I want to, but I need you," said the demon with a gleam in his eyes, revealing something reptilian behind them.

"You see, in your world I'm a heroin dealer known as Papi. I blend into my surroundings using the body of some spic I killed in an alley." The demon paused for effect, as if trying to hear his words sink in and cultivate fear in Cracky's heart. Sensing the desired effect, the demon continued its explanation. "After I donned the flesh of my victim, I began to live among your kind. For weeks I ate, breathed, and slept in your world, letting the customs and mannerisms settle upon me. Let me tell you, man, it was difficult at first, but I got the hang of it. The fucked up thing about it was the pressure of mortality on the human flesh. Holy shit was it stifling. See, your ass might not know that because you're so used to it. Oh hell, you motherfuckers are *born* with it. Yes, Death's talons gripped atop your shoulders on its perch, waiting for you to extinguish."

"What the hell does all that have to do with me?" asked Cracky angrily.

"Ah, that's a great question, friend," said the demon with a sinister smile. It cleared its throat. "You see, once I donned my prey's body, I inherited his memories, thoughts, and feelings. Let me tell you, I don't care for all that emotional mumbo jumbo. Although, fucking that guy's wife was pretty good. That's the only thing I enjoy about being human. Aside from the family bullshit, I soon discovered that my prey was a drug dealer. Not just a drug dealer, but *the* main supplier of heroin for the state of Delaware, hooking up all of the Westside Wilmington's drug dealers with what they needed to sell on the streets." The demon stopped talking for a minute to catch his breath.

"Unfortunately, though, my prey's life wasn't all fun and games. Apparently, he had fucked over the owner of the Columbian farm where the heroin was grown. Ripped off the guy for a couple million. Anyway, at the time I took over Papi's body, there was a hit out on him. Luckily, I had control over all of his memories and his thoughts and was able to hide out a bit in a small, abandoned farmhouse in New Jersey. However, the hitman caught up to me and my head was blown clean off my shoulders. Before I released my prey's body, however, I was able to open a portal to Vietnam, where I could suck up all of the hatred and injustice of war. You see, I feed off the evil that is housed in the human heart. That's how I survive in your world, and what better way to feast on hatred than in a full-scale war? That's where I found you. You're the embodiment of hate, Ron. You're just a beacon of hate, man. That's why I let myself get caught by those gooks. You were a blip on my radar, and I had to be near you. I had to feed off you to survive. In other words, I now own you, Ron. To break it down to simpler terms, you are the Renfield to my Dracula." The demon stopped speaking, then plastered a smile on its face.

"So, you mean to tell me that I'm your life source whenever you get weak?" Confusion clouded Cracky's question.

"Precisely," said the demon happily.

"Wait, if I'm your life source, wouldn't that make me your Lucy?" said Cracky, recalling the story of Dracula, remembering how the character needed to drain Lucy's blood to gain strength.

"Whatever man," said the demon, annoyed. "Look, as of right now you can kiss this military hospital goodbye. These cats will never know that you were here. Any record of you participating in this war will be gone. It will be like you never existed."

"Why me, man?" asked Cracky, still confused.

"Isn't it obvious?" said the demon. "The anger and the hatred that boils in your heart is a cauldron that holds the elixir to my immortality and independence from Satan. There's no doubt that he wants your soul, but I have you now. Now sit back and relax as I get you out of here." The demon put its hand on Cracky's forehead, spewing a strange Latin prayer.

Suddenly Cracky no longer found himself hooked up to any machines or in a hospital bed. Instead, he found himself lying on a cold concrete floor in the middle of a sidewalk, somewhere in Westside Wilmington. Gaining back his bearings, Cracky slowly stood up on patent leather shoes, with gray dress slacks and a powder blue dress shirt. With the new attire, and the stinging in his back completely gone, Cracky felt like a new man. The year was still 1965, but everything that he had lived through had completely vanished from his memories. Starting at that moment, Ron Johnson never existed as a POW in Vietnam. The lashes and scabs that scarred his back were non-existent now. It was as though he was in a brand new body. No one would fuck with him now. He felt like the fucking man. That was until he felt someone's arm wrap itself around his shoulders and pull him close.

"Welcome home, amigo." The sound of those words pierced his flesh like a thousand shards, causing him to jump in fright.

"Relax, man. You have a new and improved life."

Cracky looked to his left and saw the demon in his human form once again. This time, however, the demon wore a baby pink suit with matching patent leather shoes. The androgyny of the suit complemented its delicate, pretty boy features. Its honey brown skin was illuminated in the sun, giving its high cheekbones a healthy glow. Its hair once again was highlighted by the afternoon sun, making him look like an angel with a heavenly crown.

"Don't do that shit, man. You scared the fuck out of me," said Cracky, annoyed.

"Sorry about that, dude. I'm not used to having a partner," said the demon, smiling. "Now remember, you're my right-hand man in this drug shit, so you automatically have a target on your back, but there's no need to worry. Do you know why?" the demon paused for effect.

"What do you mean?" Cracky asked, with curiosity scrunching up his face.

"Well, because you are now the thing that is keeping me alive and giving me strength, you are now immortal." The shock of the demon's words froze Cracky in place.

"What the fuck do you mean, '*I'm immortal?*'" Without any explanation whatsoever, the demon flicked open a pocketknife and sunk its eight-inch blade deep in Cracky's gut, sending waves of sharp pain throughout his body, opening the floodgates to shock splashing around in his system.

"See, told ya," Said the demon slyly. Pulling the blade out with force, the demon showed the bloody blade off to Cracky, its sharp edges dripping with crimson. With a toothy grin that cracked the surface of its human face, the demon pointed at his gut showing him that his gut was now restored with no gash or bloodstain present.

"Nigga, did you just heal me?" asked Cracky, trying to adjust his mind to the impossible.

"No, I didn't heal you. You did that on your own. You see, you're no longer human. You have joined us demons. How can I put this delicately? Whenever I feel weak, I will feed on your soul, which means that you need to keep yourself clean, with no drugs whatsoever. In other words, you are my source of power, my source of life. Without you I'm literally nothing… just a dead leaf blowing in the wind."

Those words ran up and down Cracky's being, entering his mouth, penetrating his heart, and poisoning his soul. It was at that moment that he realized that nobody would stand in his way. He was king of the fucking world. To hell with being a weak nigga.

"Ha let's do this shit, baby!" said Cracky excitedly.

Throughout the rest of the sixties and the seventies, the demon and Cracky were the kings of smack, running the entire heroin trade for the state of Delaware and the rest of the Delmarva peninsula. However, their success didn't come without bloodshed. It didn't take long for Cracky to realize that the demon was a bit of a fuck up when it was in its human form. When the demon became Papi he was reckless, murdering anybody that got in his way without thinking about the consequences, getting himself killed numerous times. None of that mattered, however. Cracky was always there to resurrect him, but with resurrection, Cracky would lose a bit of his sanity, causing him to turn to heroin, and later, crack cocaine. He was so heavily into crack that the streets gave him his famous moniker of "Cracky" Johnson. No matter how much drugs he consumed, however, he could not make the demon's hold on him weaker. Even suicide was a failure. From hanging himself to slitting both wrists, Cracky was unable to die. It was even impossible for him to overdose. Cracky Johnson was indeed immortal.

———————

Coming down from his high, Cracky cringed at the cold January wind assaulting his senses, carrying him back to the present time of 2017. With his eyesight coming back into focus, Cracky found himself in an alley on the corner of West Fourth Street, sitting on the cold concrete with his back against a rotted wooden fence. Suddenly a large shadow blanketed Cracky, causing him to look up from his stupor. His eyes widened as he saw the demon in its human form. No longer was it looking like a suave pretty boy Puerto Rican with curly hair. Instead, what he saw in front of him was a six-foot behemoth, with thinning hair and a massive potbelly clad in a Hawaiian shirt.

"You came to kill me, motherfucker?" asked Cracky, smiling.

"Shut up, you piece of shit. You're totally useless to me now. I done told those little shits on my corners not to sell to you, but they don't listen," said the demon angrily.

"In that little corner boy's defense, he didn't sell nothing to me. I killed him and took his stuff," said Cracky nonchalantly.

"I kept you prisoner long enough, Ron. It's time that I set your useless ass free." With those words being said, a steel spike broke free from the palm of the demon's hand, penetrating Cracky's skull like a ripe honeydew melon and splattering his brains all over the rotted wooden fence. At that moment, the demon felt a wave of nausea come over itself, as if it were about to vomit. The demon wasn't ill, however; it was its body ridding itself from Cracky's soul. With blood foaming at the corners of its mouth, the demon fell on its side, grabbing its belly as it moved around in pain.

"Holy shit, this has never happened before," the demon said aloud. "Usually, when I let a soul go it's a painless experience, but this one's different." Then, it suddenly dawned on the demon. "I kept Ron's soul prisoner for far too long, which means I have become human." At this realization, the demon let out an animalistic scream that sounded through the entire neighborhood as its heart stopped. The echo of its scream rained down on Westside Wilmington.

A TALE FROM WESTSIDE WILMINGTON

CHAPTER ONE

"**Y**OU BEING RELEASED TODAY, SAMMY?" THE SOUND of my cell mate's question bounced off the concrete walls of our jail cell, riding the wave of optimism that encompassed the atmosphere around us. He knew the answer to that question, but he just liked to hear it spoken because it gave him some form of hope to latch onto.

"Yup, at 9:45 this very morning will be the last time my old Puerto Rican ass will see these walls." The words came out of my mouth with renewed optimism, as if being rinsed off by the cleansing release of a giggle.

I stood in the middle of my cell buttoning up the cuff of the left sleeve of my light blue dress shirt, trying to hold back the emotions that threatened to break free from the calm facade that I was displaying to my cell mate. Shit, I know I had every right to be at least a little emotional at that moment. I had been locked up in this bitch they call Stone Gate Prison since 1995 on some murder rap, but thanks to some strings my lawyer Donald Goldman pulled, I got the charges lowered, allowing me to serve just twenty-two years of what was once a life sentence. I don't know how he did it, but my lawyer was a fucking genius. Well, I wouldn't expect anything less from a lawyer who got reputed Italian mobsters and killers off the sights of the RICO Act.

So yeah, I had every right to shed a tear of happiness, but I wasn't going to do it in front of my cell mate. I was the guy's hero for God's sake. I didn't want to look like a pussy in front of him.

"Yo, Reggie, how I look, man?" I questioned, turning toward my cell mate on the bottom bunk.

With his hands supporting the back of his head in a nonchalant, relaxed pose, like a man who didn't have a care in the world, Reggie turned his head slowly toward me. "Man, you look like one of those White boys fresh out of college, seeking a job at one of those social media startups. Shit, with those tight ass khaki pants and light blue dress shirt you have on, who knows what you might do?" Reggie said this in between giggles.

"Fucking *maricon*," I said, waving my hand toward him in a "forget you" gesture, which prompted Reggie into a fit of laughter. His thick, baritone laughter filling up our cell somehow seemed to illuminate it, chasing away the dark and drab energy.

"Dude, all jokes aside, I wish you the best of luck out there, you hear?" I stood there and listened to him, as Reggie mustered every ounce of seriousness into his words. "I know what I just said to you came off a bit cliché, but you were given a second chance at life, which doesn't come too often for many."

Reggie was now sitting on the edge of the bottom bunk, his bare feet firmly planted on the concrete floor. He reached under his bunk without breaking from his sitting position, except for his arm that dragged out an extra-large Sava-A-Lot grocery bag that gleamed in the faint florescent lights throughout the corridor of their cell block.

I already knew what was in the bag, of course. In that grocery bag was my future. The one ticket that would redeem me from my life of crime and establish me as a fully rehabilitated member of society. Within that bag were thirty yellow legal pads worth of my story. The blue lines of every sheet in that legal pad were the veins that my story coursed through, giving birth to an entirely new perspective for my life. Yeah, I had written my autobiography and kept it in that damn shopping bag for seventeen years, and upon my release from this hell hole of a prison, I would try to get it published.

Reggie continued to speak, but this time his voice raised an octave as it began filling with emotion. "I read your whole book last week, man. Let's just say my nigga, that shit was phenomenal," he stated. His voice quivering, he now held the bag on his lap. He got up from the bed and walked toward me, holding the bag gently in his hands as though he held a precious gift sent down from the heavens. "Now, you take this manuscript and make sure that it is sent to the right people, you hear me. And don't put this masterpiece in the hands of a vanity press either. Shit, as good as that manuscript is, every reader in the world should be lining up to pay you for your book." Finishing his last words, Reggie handed me the bag and opened up his trek-riddled arms to embrace me. Those arms were a sheer reminder of Reggie's long won battle with heroin addiction. "I love you, brother, remember that. Thanks for everything you've done for me while you were in here with me."

Hearing that kind of gratitude pour so freely from the man's heart, the memory of the first time that I met him was triggered, as if someone turned on an old film projector in the theater of my mind. On its big screen, I could see a young and strung-out Reggie, whose golden-brown skin was now ashy and riddled with open scabs so fresh that some of them were a bright crimson.

"Hey man, you got a cigarette?" Reggie asked as he sat down on the bottom bunk, which as far as he was concerned was his spot for as long as he resided in prison.

"Nah, I don't smoke, man," I said to him, trying not to feel sorry for him and failing miserably. Although he was young, I couldn't help but notice that the guy reminded me of my old man. He, too, was a big-time heroin addict.

Immediately, I recalled the day that Reggie first came to prison. He arrived in a line of newbies back in 2012. It was easy to tell that he was a heroin addict by the way he jittered and shivered his way along with the other newbies. Not to mention, he was incessantly scratching his arms, where open trek wounds that resembled the mouths of tortured souls were screaming out in agony. The corrections officers who were there that day assigned me to get acclimated to the prison routine, which would spark one of the deepest friendships I ever had with any man in my life. Many nights I would hold Reggie in my arms as he withered in pain. Symptoms of heroin withdrawal ravaged his body, like a man possessed by demons. During those bouts of withdrawal, I took the time to tell him about that my life as a hit man working for Puerto Rican crime family, known as the Zepedas family; but the streets called them *Los Cucos,* or "The Boogiemen." Man, the shit I told Reggie could have landed me on death row, but I knew deep in my heart that Reggie wasn't a snitch. Plus, he knew damn well that if he snitched anything to the Cos, there would be at least twenty prisoners on *Los Cucos'* payroll that would snuff him out, no questions asked.

"Yo, thank you so much for seeing me through my withdrawals," said Reggie, breaking me out of my reveries and bringing me back to the present. "Dude, you've been a great friend to me, hell, probably the only friend that I ever had in my whole entire life," he said dramatically, tightening the grip on his hug.

"Alright, alright faggots, break it up," said a White CO sarcastically. "That's just what this world needs, a spic and a nigger trying to make babies. News flash shit heads, just cause Bruce Jenner gone up and turned hisself into a woman doesn't mean that every fag now has a uterus." The southern drawl in the CO's voice contaminated the atmosphere with its "good ol' boy" bigotry. "Let's go, Ortega, the goddamn system is setting you free."

His final comment drenched and dripping with despise, he turned the key to open my cell. Walking out of that cell for the last time, knowing deep in my heart that I would never return, felt so damn good that I didn't care if that old packer wood called me a spic. Shit, the way I saw it, I was the one leaving the clink, but that poor old overweight CO would work here until he retired or dropped dead of a heart attack. You see, the dude had no future. His best years were spent harassing prisoners.

Walking out of my cell a free man, I was ecstatic, but the cause of what put me there for twenty-two years still haunted me. It was as if my past was an evil, tormented ghost that would rear its grotesque head from the darkest depths of my soul, screaming, "You will never escape me, no matter how hard you try, motherfucker!" And at that very moment, it had its cold grip around me, bringing with it memories of that fateful day. I welcomed the bad memory to take over my thoughts right then and there. Shit, at least it helped to drown out the mindless rant of the CO as he escorted me down my final walk down the corridor of Cell Block F.

Making my way down the corridor, I was on autopilot. My body was moving forward the way any normal healthy body would, but my mind wasn't in the same place. My mind had wandered back to that crisp November night in 1995. I sat in a black Honda Accord and waited for my assignment to arrive, the car's heating system on full blast. (I hated the cooler months in Delaware, which made me desire the warmer climate of my beautiful Puerto Rico.) I looked out of my car window at the night sky that hung over the streets of Fourth and Lincoln. Hector Lavoe crooned softly from the car's stereo as I let my mind wander to the objectives of my assignment. I could see the bloated face of my boss, Israel Zepedas, as he sat behind his mahogany desk giving me the lowdown on what the assignment was about.

"This little shit they call Rico Red is said to be given intel to the authorities about our family's operation throughout the entire Eastern Shore of the US, particularly the business we got going down in Miami with the Dominicans and Haitians, and the young boy Rico was supposed to be the representative for the Zepedas family as their heroine distributor through-out Delaware. In other words, Rico would go down to Miami and pick up an amount of heroin and bring it up to Delaware via speed boat. It sounds simple enough, right? But no, that stupid little shit put the cops on to the entire operation. So, that's where I came in. I was the custodian to clean up their mess. Rico Red had to be dealt with like any other snitch: a bullet to the head."

The digital clock on my dashboard read 10:45 p.m. when I saw Rico's white Benz park behind my Honda from my rear-view mirror, the custom gold Mercedes logo glinting a faint orange glow from the streetlights.

"About fucking time this nigga show up, damn," I said, watching as my target got out of his car. I had to admit, I had no love for Rico, and would have gladly done his ass in for free. Shit, the fact that I was getting paid to kill the motherfucker was just a bonus on my view.

I watched him as his red leather-clad body opened the passenger side door to my car and sat in the seat. I remember thinking to myself, *who does this nigga think he is, Eddie Murphy fresh off his* Delirious *comedy special?*

"What up, man?" said Rico, giving me dap with a big corny-looking grin plastered on his face.

"Dude, what the fuck is up with that tight ass red jumpsuit you have on? You look retarded as hell," I said in between giggles.

"Nigga, why are you hating on me, man? Shit, I gots to look good for the type of money I be pulling in," said Rico in his thick Dominican accent.

Truth be told, the dude thought he was hot shit and was very flamboyant when it came to his style. Whether it was the way he dressed or his attitude, dude thought he was "Big Time" and that was his downfall. Or so I thought.

"So, you're the cat the boss sent to check out the product I picked up from Miami, eh?"

Shocked at the redundant the question sounded, I answered, "You see me here driving this car, don't you, dumbass?"

As my statement took its full-blown effect on Rico's ego, I looked at him from the corner of my eye. It was then that I became aware of how ridiculous the guy looked. His hair was fashioned in the style of a pompadour of the early 1960s. His ear lobes donned ruby-studded earrings with a pair of ruby-studded sunglasses to match, glinting each time we passed a streetlamp.

"Damn nigga, who do you think you are, Elton John?" I said, as the bile of disgust began to raise in the back of my throat. That's what I hated most about the young cats coming up in the game when I was in the streets. They would come into a little bit of dough and suddenly they were buying expensive cars, jewelry, and an outlandish wardrobe. Meanwhile, those cats didn't have a pot to piss in because they still lived in their mamma's basement, and that was the case with Rico Red.

"Ah I see how it is, man, you just hating on 'cause you can't get shit right like me," he said. I could feel Rico's spiteful smile on me as looked straight ahead on the road as I drove. His cocky smile was digging into me and grating my last nerve. *I'm going to enjoy killing this piece of shit,* I thought. I drove in silence the entire way to Rico's stash house house as he bragged about having two side chicks and a "really good bitch" at home that didn't suspect a thing about his endeavors with the other two woman.

"Yeah, you the man," I said, not really focusing on the garbage he was spewing.

"Dude, turn left right here," said Rico, pointing toward a self-storage facility off the site of the road.

"Why the fuck do you have the product stashed away in a place like this?" I asked, pulling up to a chain link security gate that had keypad that stood on a steel pole right beside it. When a person drove up, they would be able to punch in their entrance code from the driver side window.

"I'm gonna need your code, man," I said to Rico as I stopped the car in front of the keypad.

"It's one five seventy-six," he responded, with a huge grin that revealed a set of gold front teeth. "That's my date of birth you just punched in." His voice held a tinge of pride, as if to convey his cleverness to me.

Jesus, he's just a kid, I thought as I watched the gate slowly open on its pulleys. *Oh well, he shouldn't have been playing a grown man's game. He knew what the consequences were if he fucked up. He is just arrogant.* These thoughts raced through my mind as my Honda rounded a corner. The street was filled what seemed to be small and medium-sized garages stacked side-by-side like row homes in a ghetto, each with a bright orange door complete with padlocks.

"Those three storage containers are where I keep the product," said Rico, pointing out the final three storage sheds to the left of the parking lot. "Just park next to them and then we can get down to business." *Was this nigga for real?* Was this guy stashing away heroin in a place where there were surveillance cameras? This motherfucker was stupid, no doubt, but I was the one with the dunce cap that night. As it turned out, the kid had on a wire. So, when I parked the car, quickly pulled out my gun, and shot the bastard through the right temple (at the same time thinking about breaking into the storage facility's main office and steal the night's surveillance tape), I heard the wailing of police sirens.

Suddenly, two paddy wagons blocked my escape: one in the front and one in the back. In addition, five Delaware State Police cars were blocking the exit to the storage facility. In my moment of desperation, I ran from the car and blacked out. When I came to, I was in the hospital, hooked up to all kinds of monitors and shit. Apparently, those fucking cops shot me up something serious because I was in a coma for two-and-a-half months. When I regained my full health back, however, I stood trial and was convicted of murder of the first degree, which my lawyer overturned. It took him twenty-two years, but the man did the damn thing.

"Look alive there, Ortega!" the CO barked, pulling me back to the present.

Shaking the cobwebs from my thoughts, I realized that I was standing in front of a plexiglass window with a slender, middle-aged Black CO behind it. Boredom seemed to be permanently embedded in his demeanor, his bald head shining from the naked bulb above him. Strangely enough, I could see that the guy's lips were moving, but all I could hear was

jumbled mumbling as he handed me the items, they had con-
fiscated from me twenty-two years ago.

"Good luck to you, Mr. Ortega," he said, as if he was some
amateur actor reading the line from a play in front of a crowd.

"Thanks, man," I said, my eyes transfixed on the man's
shiny head. It was as though he had a halo, and I was drawn
to it.

I grabbed my bag, watching the man press a button to
unlock the exit. Since the exit was on an automatic switch,
it slowly flung itself open, releasing what seemed to be
compressed air from the electric hinges. Wasting no time, I
walked at a brisk pace toward the rays of sunshine, thinking
they looked like a dead body splayed out on the floor. Oddly
enough, as I walked out of that hell hole, I looked behind me
and saw my elongated shadow spilled across the floor, swallowing up the sunshine that was once in its place.

CHAPTER TWO

TAKING MY FIRST STEPS OUT OF STONE GATE, THE FIRST thing that I felt was a strong, cool wind caressing my face and the backs of my hands, as if it was an old friend welcoming me back home. However, I put all of that poetic bullshit out of my mind because the first thing I saw when I looked to my left was a 2017 Mercedes XL, which had ridiculous looking chrome rims. I sighed in disgust. "I swear, cats spend their money on the most frivolous things these days," I mumbled under my breath as I moved toward it. The dark green paint job on the car screamed it's a new day as the morning sunlight bounced off its rims, almost blinding me. The Mercedes logo stood proudly on head of the car's hood, gleaming in the sun, as if saying, "Yeah, nigga, I got money."

I shook my head at this false symbol of power and wealth. What a false god it was to all of us cats trying to come up in the hood. Shaking my head I thought, *You know how many dudes I killed inside Benzes like this one right here? Shit, I done lost count of the bodies. The sad thing is, however, the devil ain't gonna let nobody drive a Benz in his hood, you know what I'm saying?*

"What up, Sammy?" exclaimed a male voice from the lowered window of the Benz.

I walked over to the car and poked my head into the gap the passenger side window was supposed to occupy. It was then that I realized my lawyer, Donald Goldman, was behind the wheel of that gaudy-looking Benz. Truth be told, I wasn't expecting him to be there, but there he was. Not only was he there but he was dressed in full street clothes, complete with an oversized white Yankees T-shirt and Timberland boots. From a simple glance, one wouldn't figure the guy driving that Benz to be one of the top criminal lawyers in Delaware, but I guess Goldman was the epitome of the old phase "Don't judge a book by its cover." Although only thirty years old, Donald Goldman was considered one of the most brilliant lawyers in America, winning the respect of a lot of his colleagues and the hatred of those who opposed him; for those who opposed him knew that he had Mafia and low-level street organizations. Goldman, however, didn't give a fuck what his colleagues thought about him. The way he saw it, they weren't the ones paying his bills and child support.

"What are you doing here, man?" I asked surprised, with a big grin plastered on my face.

"I came to give you a ride in my new joint," he said.

It's funny, but if I closed my eyes at that moment, I'd swear I was talking to my homies from around the way. It didn't matter that Donald was a White boy with a Princeton education, he was down as fuck when it came to handling shit. So yeah, dude got his hood pass. I got in his car, smelling the newness of its cream leather interior as the cool breath of the AC blasted in my face. Shutting the passenger door, I began to notice the heat that started to sting my backside.

"Damn nigga, did you really have to get leather seats?! They're scolding hot in the summer," I whined.

He smiled, pressing play on the car's CD player, and said, "Quit whining man, ain't you supposed to be a stone-cold killer?"

I gave him a dirty look as if to say, *Shut the fuck up, bitch. I will break your face.* He must have read the look on my face correctly because the smile was instantly gone from his face and replaced with fear. It was then that I got my first taste of twenty-first century hip-hop music. *"Raindrops drop tops/smoking a spliff in a hot box."* My ears couldn't believe the stupid shit that was coming out of the radio.

"Yo, what the fuck is playing on the radio, B?"

Donald looked at me in horror and began to stutter. "Um, it's, ah…Migos."

Ha, I swear, I could literally see the nigga shit his pants. "Dude, is this how all hip-hop music sounds nowadays?" I asked, catching a hint of despair in my voice and hating it.

"Yup, pretty much, but there are still some truly deep lyricists. For example, you got this cat from Compton who calls himself Kendrick Lamar. There's also another cat that goes by the name of J. Cole, but I forgot what city he reps."

Not caring about much for what he was saying, I asked if he had Nas's *Illmatic*. Without responding to my question, he let out a sigh and said, "Siri, play Nas's *Illmatic*." At his request, the opening track began to play, bouncing off the speakers of the car.

"Now that's what the fuck I'm talking about," I exclaimed happily, listening to the track titled *Genesis*.

"What's with the shopping bag?" asked Goldman, nodding at the Save-A-Lot that rested on the floor of his car.

"Just a little book I wrote," I responded nonchalantly.

"Man, you were steady writing in the clink, huh," said Goldman, curiosity overtaking him. There was a moment of silence between us. The only sound in the car was Nas and

AZ rapping about how life was a bitch. Clearing his throat nervously, Goldman broke the silence.

"You didn't write about your case, did you?" Goldman's voice was filled with apprehension and fear, which caused me to let out a giggle.

"Nah man, you straight, there ain't nothing about you in my book. That shit just talks about my past in the streets," I said, watching Goldman exhale a sigh of relief.

The rest of the ride home was encompassed in a thick silence, which allowed me to go deep into my thoughts. Lost in the halls of my psyche, I arrived at a section that housed memories of Sheila Jade, my wife. Just thinking of her mocha-colored skin pressed against mine would drive me to the edge of madness when I was in prison. At night, when sleep failed to sit upon my eyelids, my soul ran wild within the museum of my mind, allowing me to stand in front of portraits of her. Yeah, my queen. The one and only woman that could silence the screaming demons that ran wild throughout the valleys of my mind and soul. The woman who noticed that I was human way before I did, or anyone else for that matter. If there's one thing that I thank God for, it's the fact that Sheila is in my life. She has been the closest thing to purity.

"Tell me something Sammy, how does a stone-cold killer be such a romantic and sensitive poet at the same time?" said Donald, as if reading my mind.

Caught off guard by his comment, I looked at him with an inquisitive glance and said, "What the hell you talking about, bro?"

That's when Goldman's face split into a somewhat grotesque smile. He said, "During your last trial, Sheila came to court with a composition book full of poems that you had written to her back in the day. My dude, I gotta say, them shits were sappier than a motherfucker. However, I don't blame you." He paused. "Shit, no offense, but Sheila's sexier than a motherfucker. Man, if my bitch looked like her, I'd be one happy Jewish boy."

Hearing those words come out of his mouth made my blood boil and my fists and jaw clench. I couldn't stand anyone seeing the love of my life as a piece of meat. God knows there are niggas like that, but I've come to the realization that the reason why some dudes act like that toward women is because they haven't felt the true feelings of being in love, as cliché as that sounds. Yeah, a woman becomes more than a woman when she awakens your heart from a deep dark slumber with her love. Noticing the mixture of anger and disgust on my face, Goldman nervously cleared his throat and quickly changed the subject back to my poetry.

"So, how long have been writing?" By the sound of his voice, I knew that he asked the question out of genuine curiosity, and not as a method or tool for clowning me.

"Shit, I've been writing stuff here and there since I was a little runt running crazy in the streets, you know," I said nonchalantly. "Writing down my thoughts and emotions kept me sane. I guess you can say it kept my humanity intact."

Goldman let out a deep sigh and said, "Damn, playa, that's some seriously deep shit."

No more was said between us the rest of the ride home. Nas was the only one talking at the moment, by way of the iPod hooked up to my dude's radio. He exclaimed, "The world is mine!"

CHAPTER THREE

AS WE APPROACHED THE OFF RAMP OF I-95, I COULD make out the green-tiled roof of St. Paul Church, its gray stone facade looking like a castle from the Middle Ages somehow smack dab in the middle of the ghetto. Oddly enough, I always thought of that church as a sign that I was home, a beacon that emphasized the fact that I made it home safely from whatever job or journey I was on.

"Damn, ain't nothing change about Wilmington the last twenty years, I see!" I exclaimed to no one in particular, eyeing the streets below the interstate where the moving cars and people looked like tiny insects.

"Nah, not much has changed in the city, but they have torn down some old row homes and a few buildings to make room for brand new town houses. Welcome to the era of gentrification, my friend," Goldman said in a Spanish accent that I found a bit offensive.

"Let me get this straight, the government is tearing down the hood and putting up homes that cost a mint for White people to buy? Ain't that some shit, whites taking back the hood." Shaking my head in disgust, I couldn't help but see the irony.

"Come on, man, it's not like the people that lived in those homes weren't paid off by the government," said Goldman defensively.

I couldn't help but shake my head at his response. "No offense, but you are drowning in White Ignorance. Don't you see, even if the government did pay those people off, they still wouldn't give the owner of the house the correct amount the property is worth."

Goldman frowned at this statement and said, "Who died and made you a real estate lawyer?"

I didn't dignify his dumbass question with an answer and just looked out my window, letting my blood simmer down. We were now approaching my block, Fourth and Jackson. The row homes on either side of the block's two sidewalks stood tall, like multiple conjoined twins, giants petrified by the passage of time and turned to brick. I could now see the entire left side of St. Paul Church, its stone facade surrounded by a black steel fence that led to an entrance gate to the courtyard. *Damn, that place never changes,* I thought. Yup, my ass was definitely home.

"Yo, pull up to the house with the fenced-in front porch," I said to Goldman, pointing out my house. Feeling the excitement surge through my body, I could hardly contain myself, and jumped out of the car before it was fully parked.

"Damn, motherfucker, hold your horses," Goldman said between giggles. Without saying my goodbyes to him, I ran toward the house like a young child coming home on his last day of school. I didn't even make it to the steps when I realized that the front door flew open and Sheila came running down the steps, her silky dark brown hair flowing behind her as she ran toward me. Her torso hugged tightly by a white tank top, emphasizing her C-cup breasts. I couldn't help but feel my manhood stiffen. She didn't help matters with her tight ass jeans either. Good God almighty!

Without any formal greeting passed between us, Sheila ran into my arms, pressing her plump, moist lips to mine. I kid you not, we lasted in that particular embrace for at least five minutes. It was as though our bodies and souls hungered for each other. Tears began to stream down our cheeks as we stopped kissing. It was as though our souls were escaping the confines of our bodies to properly greet one another. As if to appease that very desire, I put my tear-streaked face against hers, allowing our fresh tears to mingle. Two souls had become one once again. At that particular moment, the world seemed to fade all around us. It was just us, and nothing else in the world mattered. The world could have come crumbling down around us and we would be safe in each other's arms.

"Sammy, don't forget your shit, man!" Goldman yelled from his driver's side window, holding out my bag. As if awakening from a trance, I wiped my eyes and shook the cobwebs from my head, breaking away from Sheila's embrace to run toward Goldman's car. Grabbing the bag from his outstretched hand, I could hear him laughing to himself. "My dude, you're the softest son of a bitch I know," he said.

"Whatever nigga," I responded, not even giving him a glance as I turned back toward Sheila.

"Have a nice life, Sammy." Goldman's words were barely audible now over the purring of the Benz's engine. In response to his bland goodbye, I made a peace sign with my right hand as I walked away.

Entering the house, my sense of smell was overcome with the aroma of Puerto Rican food. My mouth began to water as that smell conjured up images of my favorite dishes. I knew that red rice with chickpeas was cooking on the stove, *arroz con gandules,* as it is known in Spanish. My stomach began to roar with hunger. It was as though I hadn't eaten in the past twenty-two years. Shit, you gotta understand, I was kept all those years from eating a home-cooked meal. As if in a trance, I let myself be guided by the sweet aroma that was coming from the kitchen.

Entering it, I found a short elderly woman in front of the stove, a neat little gray bun sat atop her head. She wore an old yellow flower print dress that hung loose on her body. She clearly had lost a tremendous amount of weight. My heart sank as I suddenly realized who that old woman at the stove was. It was none other than good ole Mami Yadi, or Mamma Yadi to Black kids in the neighborhood. Mami Yadi was the woman who raised Sheila throughout her teenage years taking her in after the sudden, and well-deserved, death of Sheila's stepdad. Even though there wasn't any blood relation between the two women, Mami Yadi was the only mother figure that Sheila ever had in her life. Mami Yadi was considered to be the hood's mother. She fed and even clothed all the kids in the neighborhood. She didn't care if you were Black, White, Latin or a two-headed purple alien from Mars, she showed you all the love in the world. When I was growing up, there was a rumor going around that the reason why Mami Yadi cared for the kids in the neighborhood was because she was barren, which was a shame because she would have been a great mother.

"Mami Yadi, is that you, girl?" I said this in a playful tone to generate a reaction from her.

She turned away from the stove with a hand on her hip, gyrating it in a come-hither fashion.

"Why hello there, Sammy, long time no see." She couldn't keep up the joke much longer and stopped her gyration, letting laughter release in the form of a deep hearty bellow. "How are you, *mi amor?*" Mami Yadi held out her arms for me to walk into her embrace. I can't lie, walking into her felt like I was being reunited with my mom after not seeing her for twenty-two years. (She visited me once when I was locked up, but I told her not to visit me again because I hated the fact that she had to see me in prison.) As a matter of fact, she was the only mother figure I knew growing up. I guess that's what happens when you're found abandoned in a dumpster when you're an infant.

I wasn't adopted by Mami Yadi, though. Instead, I was put in a foster home when I was ten. Don't get it twisted, though; the foster home I grew up in wasn't your average home either. It was run by this cat named Carter Johnson. At the time I was there, Carter had at least six kids living in his home, all of whom were males of the Black and Latino persuasion. Carter, though, wasn't a fatherly figure. He taught us how to be killers, hustlers, and con artists. He taught me all that there was to be a hitman. Man, Carter would be pissed if he knew how I fucked up Rico Red's murder.

"I see you're still prone to zoning out," Mami Yadi said sarcastically, pulling me away from the memory of Carter.

"What?" I asked a bit disoriented.

"Where's Sheila? I thought I heard her come in the house." I could hear a bit of annoyance start to simmer in her question, which she might have asked numerous times.

"My bad, Mami. I think she's upstairs." I answered her with a smile, hoping that my zoning out didn't piss her off too much.

"*Papito,* do me a favor and tell Sheila that the food's ready," said Mami Yadi as she busied herself at the stove with a frying pan.

Making my way up the second floor, I felt out of place, as if my ass didn't belong there. It was like some surreal feeling within my entire being nagging at me that I didn't belong anywhere; that I should go away and leave Mami Yadi and Sheila alone and not fuck up their lives. As this thought slowly began to fade from my mind, I made my way toward Sheila's bedroom, but I froze in the doorway when I saw her sitting at the foot of the queen-sized bed reading one of my yellow legal pads with the rest of them beside her. I totally forgot about my book as soon as I entered the house.

"What do you think about it so far?" The sound of my question seemed to shatter the thick silence that encompassed the room.

Without even flinching, my baby girl looked at me and said, "Look at you on your Donald Goines shit," she said, getting up from the bed and putting her arms around me. I let my hands roam around the curves of her body as our tongues danced with one another. "Let me type that up for you on my laptop, *Papi,* I think it has the potential to be a *New York Times Bestseller.*"

"You really think so, ma?" I asked, fishing for a response. Hell yeah, cats eat that shit up, especially with the title that you gave it." To be real with you, I thought *Confessions of a Street Soldier* was a whack title for the book, but if Sheila was rocking with it, then it was cool.

CHAPTER FOUR

THE SMELL OF SEX PERMEATED THE WALLS OF THE ROOM, drowning out the smell of Mami Yadi's red rice and chickpeas. I lay naked in between the sheets beside Sheila, watching her sleep. Her beautiful face was in total relaxation at the moment, letting me know that she was at peace for now. Although she was thirty-nine years old, Ma didn't look a day over twenty-five. Her caramel complexion did not have a single wrinkle. Plus, her body was still on point, rivaling any video vixen out there. "Puerto Rican don't crack, baby," I whispered to myself, softly giggling. She was my angel, my queen, the whole reason why I still had my humanity.

At that moment, memories of the first time we met began to flood my mind, putting me into the shoes of my thirteen-year-old self on that hot late August at Camby pool, a community pool that kids all over the ghetto frequented every summer until it shut down in the midnineties. That's where me and my nigga Ace would sell weed and make a hell of a profit, too.

"Man, it's hot as hell out here," complained Ace as he took off his plain white T-shirt.

"Shit, you ain't lying, I'm 'bout to jump in that pool my damn self," I replied. I watched as Ace made his way to a row of trees where a bench and a metal trash can were underneath. Hiding what was left of the weed we were selling underneath the trash can, we went to the gigantic Olympic-sized swimming pool that was teeming with kids.

Noticing that Ace had his shirt draped on one of his shoulders, I decided to bust his balls. "Dude, ain't you scared of getting sunburned?"

He responded to me with a snort of laughter. "Nigga, you stupid…don't you know that I have melanin in my skin? It protects me from getting sunburned. That's one of the perks of being dark-skinned. Not to mention that dark-skinned niggas been in high demand ever since Wesley Snipes did his thing in *New Jack City.* Shit, bitches can't keep they hands off after they saw that movie. Ha, sometimes I gotta beat the pussy off me with a stick," bragged Ace, popping an invisible collar from his exposed collarbone.

As if on cue, a chick's voice yelled out, "Ace, don't act like you don't know me, nigga!" Those words froze Ace in his tracks, as if the words were shot from a ray gun that paralyzed every muscle in his body and freezing him in place. Out of nowhere came a beautiful dark-skinned girl who smacked the shit out of Ace, her hand making a grotesque suction sound as it connected with his face.

"Why did you dog me out like that, motherfucker?!" the girl cried, her young breast heaving up and down in anger. Ace's eyes flooded with anger, but he never advanced toward her. Ace was no saint by any means, but any other dude would have fucked the chick up really good. Carter, however, taught us well. At that moment I could literally hear Carter's teaching pass right through his head, as if it were from Sound Cloud. *"Despite how much a woman may anger you, never raise a hand to harm her. A man who raises his hand to a woman is nothing but a coward, a bitch-ass nigga. Remember, your hands were made for war but never to bring harm to our queens."*

"Damn, Chardey, why the fuck you do that for?" cried Ace, his open palms covering his face against Chardey's attacks.

"Nigga, quit acting brand new. You know you fucked up, but what was I expecting from a guy who has a reputation like yours?"

As much as I loved Ace, I had to admit that he was somewhat of a dog with the ladies. I had no idea what Ace did to that girl, but more than likely, he got her to fuck him, suck him off, or both. And knowing Ace the way I did, he probably got what he wanted and bounced.

"You ain't nothing but a piece of shit, you inconsiderate bastard!" Chardey yelled at the top of her lungs. The chick was so angry that her whole body shook uncontrollably, as if she were about to explode. "How could you do that to me, Patrick?!"

Ace rolled his eyes, annoyed that Chardey had called him by his real name. "Bitch, why you out here calling me by my government name, you should know better than that." He sounded like an angry father berating his little girl. Chardey's beautiful facial features were instantly pulled down by the weight of a frown, which strangely seemed to enhance her beauty. I mean, the girl was gorgeous, looking all cute in her two-piece neon red bathing suit.

Truth be told, I wasn't feeling the way Ace was treating Chardey. In my opinion, a chick that beautiful deserved to be treated like a queen, but Ace was the fuck-them-and-leave-them type of dude; that's where him and I differed, but who was I to judge?

"Chardey, what is up with you, girl?" said a woman's voice as it floated on the wave of an echo in our direction. I swear, the ears to my soul perked up, causing my heart to awaken from a long slumber. *Where the hell is that beautiful voice coming from*? I thought. My eyes desperately searched for the owner of that sweet voice. "Yo, what is up with you, nigga? You acting all disoriented, like a lost puppy or some shit," exclaimed Ace, a mixture of exasperation and disgust in his voice. Meanwhile, tears were streaming down Chardey's face. "Man, let's fucking bounce."

"Yo, what the fuck y'all do to my girl?" My heart began to pound in my chest like crazy, as if a madman was bouncing off the padded walls of his cell. I just had to find out who that beautiful voice belonged to. My heart now controlling the movement of my body, I quickly turned right back around.

Now, holding Chardey in a consoling embrace, was a mocha-skinned girl in a turquoise one-piece bathing suit. Her hair was long and curly, and when the sun hit it just right, you could see that it was a deep shade of brown. Her eyes were almond shaped, almost catlike, which brought out the honey brown and hint of lavender that decorated her irises. Her beautiful pouty lips drove me wild; I had to restrain the urge to kiss them. On the real, I had never in my life seen a girl so beautiful, and I don't care how cliché that shit sounds. Babygirl had a nigga going.

"I asked y'all motherfuckers a question. What did y'all do to my girl?" The question came with more fire and feistiness behind it.

"First off, woman, you need to calm the fuck down," said Ace. His comment was the lighter fluid that strengthened the flame of her anger.

She walked toward him with a sarcastic smile and said between clenched teeth, "I am not your woman!"

Seeing how angry she was, a smile broke the angry scowl that had masked his face. "Chill ma…you're too pretty to scuffle."

In response to Ace's comment, the girl connected her knee with his groin, causing him to grab himself and howl in pain.

"Let's go. I think we've played enough games with these assholes," said the girl who came to Chardey's rescue, putting her arm around her and walking her away.

"Man, why the fuck you smiling for, nigga?" asked Ace, directing his anger at me.

"On the real my dude, you brought that shit onto yourself," I said in between giggles.

"Yeah, fuck you then, nigga," Ace countered while he retrieved our stash of weed from the metal trash can beside the bench.

"If I didn't know any better, I'd say that your dumbass is in love with that stuck up little Spanish bitch," he said, giving me the dirtiest look I have ever seen in my life. "First off, you need to stop playing around with females the way you do. Second, you should know that Spanish broads don't take no shit from nobody." Ace dismissed what I was saying with a quick "forget you" wave of his hand and laughed. "What you know about that, nigga, you ain't never had no chicks. Come to think of it, I know for a fact that you're still a virgin, nigga."

As he made fun of me, I couldn't help but wonder what that girl's name was. *What was a girl that beautiful doing in the in a place like Wilmington, Delaware?* Don't get a nigga wrong. I'm not saying that my hometown doesn't produce beautiful women, but there was something different about this chick that was invading my mind and heart. She was like an exotic creature that was rare to see in this part of the world. For the brief minutes that was our first encounter, my soul was suffering from a divine hunger and thirst so profound, I just had to see her again.

"Yo dogg, you know that Spanish broad's name?" I asked, interrupting Ace's incessant rambling.

"Ha, I knew it, bitch got you sprung!"

Hearing him call the girl a bitch infuriated me, causing my teeth to clench and my fists to ball. Word on everything, I was ready to fight that nigga for the first time in our friendship.

"Don't call her a bitch, homie," I said, anger boiling through my veins.

Looking at me from head to toe, Ace scrunched up his face and jeered, "Nigga, you are so soft that it's ridiculous. Shit, that's not how Carter raised us to be. We're supposed to be street soldiers, men who fight for the betterment of themselves without the binding of any laws whatsoever."

What came to mind at that moment was that Ace had rehearsed that shit he just spewed. It was like he studied Carter's teachings to a tee but didn't put them into practice.

"Ah, but Carter also taught us that we should respect females, for they're our mothers, sisters, and future daughters. Remember, he who doesn't respect females doesn't respect life itself, because females are the portals of all human life. In other words, without women we wouldn't exist. Therefore, we owe them the ultimate respect." I wasn't just saying that. I spoke from the heart, and Ace knew that.

"Whatever, nigga, you're just saying that because that Spanish chick got your dick all hard and shit." Ace opened the front door to our house where we lived with Carter, our foster father on the eleven hundred block of Lancaster Avenue. Ace carried on with his jeering until we stepped through the front door and saw Carter sitting across the living room on the old rose-print sofa, the kind usually associated with an old lady's home. He sat in the middle with his legs open sporting black basketball shorts with a white tank top embossed with a neon red Nike logo. His dark brown, hairless scalp shone brilliantly against the light fixture above his head, making him look like some of hood saint.

"What are you little niggas babbling about?" Carter asked, taking his attention away from the book he was reading and focusing on us.

"Sammy's in love," said Ace in a high-pitched girly voice, batting his eyelashes. I could feel my face redden, thinking that Carter would view me as weak for expressing emotions. Instead, to my surprise, Carter's face split into a grin, one mimicking the smile of that creepy feline from *Alice in Wonderland*. His eyes shone with glee, as if he had spent years yearning to witness one of his foster children fall in love. However, his smile faded as quickly as it spread on his face.

"Y'all little niggas got my money?" Carter asked, with the seriousness of a doctor who was telling his patient that they had cancer.

"Yeah man, we got your dough," said Ace, his voice a deep timbre of confidence. He dug in his jeans pockets and handed Carter a wad of money. I could see Carter's eyes scrutinizing the size of the money stack.

"Y'all niggas came up a bit short today, huh?" he sighed in disgust. Despite his slight disappointment, however, he pocketed the money.

Seeing this, Ace transformed into defensive mode. "Man, you know them little shits at Camby Pool ain't got nothing but fucking milk money. Shit, we're lucky if we get a customer that spends twenty dollars on this shit!" Ace yelled with a full force of anger that he previously held back during his argument with Chardey and the Spanish chick. The dark cloud of a scowl took over Carter's face, as if he was a sniper positioning the little red dot of his rifle on his target. Without a single word, Carter jumped from the sofa and punched Ace square in the jaw, causing the boy to reel back and fall to the floor, clutching his jaw.

"You better come correct when you step to me with all that crazy back talk, boy!"

Wide-eyed with fear and shock, Ace got on his feet and walked up to Carter with his head down, mumbling that he was sorry. Carter nodded his head in response to Ace's apology, as if to say that he was forgiven for his rudeness. Still rubbing the left side of his jaw, Ace walked upstairs to the room we both shared.

"Sammy, go upstairs and try to talk some sense into Ace. That little nigga has lost his goddamn mind. Little shit is feeling himself, huh?"

Without saying a word, I headed upstairs and directly to my room. As soon as I entered, I was greeted by the sound of a punching bag being hit repeatedly. On the real, though, I could have cared less about Ace's current issue with Carter. Ace was always getting himself into shit. Man, most of the time he got what he deserved.

"Carter be on some bullshit!" Ace whined as he pounded heavily on the punching bag. "Nigga better slow his roll, you know what I'm saying?"

On the real, though, my ass didn't care what he was saying. I was too preoccupied with thoughts of Chardey's homegirl. My mind kept going back to her feisty attitude and the way she defended Chardey against Ace's rudeness. Hell, I loved how I got to witness that, a strong-minded Spanish broad. Shit, at the time, the Spanish broads that I encountered were usually overly submissive with men, obeying the will of just about every man that they came across. That wasn't the case with this chick, however. Nah, this one wasn't going to lie down and let dudes trample all over her. She was going to let herself be heard, felt, and feared. Goddamn, that was some kind of broad. Shit, I just knew right then and there that I needed to be with her, surrounding myself with the beauty that was her. On the real, I thought love was some fairytale shit that you see in a fucking Disney flick, but that hot August day in 1990 gave me a whole new perspective on what the love and courage of a strong-minded female really were. As cliché as that might sound, that was my introduction to love, making a human being.

As the summer drew on, I had no contact whatsoever with the Spanish beauty that was now the queen of my heart. Every day I would go to Camby Pool, making my rounds, selling weed and checking for my queen, but she was nowhere to be found, which would send my mind into full-on poet mode.

"Nigga, you need to erase that bitch from your mind, otherwise you're going to make yourself sick in the head." Ace would say this whenever he saw me writing a poem at my desk. Of course, I would shake off his comments because I knew that he didn't know what it felt like to be in love. "Nigga, that ain't love, that's called obsession."

I shook my head defiantly, without turning away from what I was writing, and said, "If you only open the doors to your heart, you would know exactly how I feel."

Sucking his teeth, Ace responded, "Man, fuck all that faggot bullshit you be on."

One night, as I was finishing up my umpteenth love poem of the summer, Carter walked in and pulled up a chair beside me. He wore a white wife beater with a pair of baggy jeans and Timberland boots. His forearms bulged, signs of a dude who lifted a large number of weights on a daily basis. He said, "Little nigga, what's this I hear about you tripping over some chick you met at Camby's?"

Carter's question caught me a bit off guard, which must have shown on my face. He had a grin on his face that reminded me of Ace when he knew a big secret and wasn't telling me.

"I don't know what you're talking about, man," I said, thinking I could get one past Carter.

His right fist came out of nowhere and connected with my jaw, knocking me to the floor. "Why you gotta lie to me, nigga?!" His voice seemed to form a sonic blast as he stood over me.

Trying to stop my head from spinning, I managed to pick myself up off the floor and stand before him, with burning coals of anger shining brightly in my eyes.

"Oh, so you pissed now, huh," Carter mocked, getting into a fighting stance. "Come at me then, nigga."

Shit, I knew what time it was.

Suddenly, Carter came at me with the fury of a hurricane, forcing me to duck to prevent getting a swift kick to the head. He then proceeded to attack with a succession of rapid punches to my body and face, which I expertly blocked. Noting that there was an opening to attack his midsection, I let of a succession of punches, knocking the wind out of Carter.

Noticing that he was in a daze, I quickly jumped up and connected two swift roundhouse kicks to Carter's face, causing him to land hard on my desk which caved in on its four legs. Watching my desk collapse under Carter was the shit to me. It meant that from that moment on, I was to be respected by him, and it also meant I was officially a man that could hold my own in this cold, cruel world.

Walking toward his laid-out body, I braced myself for anything, keeping my guard up. Knowing that motherfucker like I did, I was prepared for any unexpected attack that he would most likely throw at me.

"Rule number one," Carter would often say during our training, "Don't underestimate your opponent when he's down. Remember, your opponent will use the fact that he is down to lure you in for a sneak attack, and then kill you. Always keep your guard up no matter what."

Shit, and best believe that my ass took that to heart at that moment I approached his sprawled-out body on that broken desk. To my surprise, though, he didn't sneak attack me. Instead, he smiled at me, looking like some hungover vampire with extremely bloody fangs.

"Damn little nigga, I taught you well," said Carter, his hand on his lower back, trying miserably to relieve the pain. "Let me get cleaned up and we'll talk about this chick that got you going all crazy." He rubbed his lower back, slowly walking out of my room as if he was a decrepit, hunched over old man.

After getting cleaned up and in his blue terrycloth robe, Carter met me at the dining room table, a small wooden round thing that symbolized the poverty that we were living in. Scuff marks suggested that it had seen better days. We didn't care, though. Shit, that was the table that we told our secrets at. Many a person's fate was decided at that table. Hell, even blood and pieces of brains were splattered on its surface every once in a while, but at that particular moment that table was holding count of matters of the heart. Carter sat down in one of the rickety old wooden chairs that served as a seat for the dining room table, creaking under his weight.

"What's this I hear about you falling head over heels over some little broad you met at Camby's?" Carter asked, stone-faced. I was too scared to answer.

"Look, don't get me wrong, it's cool to fall in love, but you can't let it blind you to the point of obsession. Once you do that you will become weak in all aspects of your person. Meaning that if you obsess over love, your mind, body, and spirit will become distorted, allowing your enemies to overrun you and take what is yours. Remember, I raised you to be a soldier because we are in battle with this White man's world, so I raised you to get by in it by any means necessary. Shit, even if it means that you gotta catch a body. Don't let that little chick be your downfall. Don't let her be the Eve to your Adam, you understand what I'm saying to you, nigga?"

"I get what you're saying, but I never thought that that any human emotion like this ever existed," I said. Carter gave me a strange look. "I know this shit that I am telling you might sound cliché, but just the sound of that girl's voice seemed to cleanse my soul. It was as if at that moment, when her voice struck my eardrums, my heart was awakened from a deep slumber, showing me that there was a part of me that was missing. Do you know what I mean, man?"

Carter nodded his head solemnly, letting each word I said sink in. That was when I noticed a single tear drop sliding down his left cheek, shocking the fuck out of me. Seeing him cry for the first time was like watching a god break down at my feet. Shit like that never happened. Carter was a cold-blooded killer who dedicated his life to molding future killers. He wasn't the type of nigga who showed his emotions. He was the type of cat to use his emotions as fuel to enhance physical training to become a better killer.

"You see this damn tear coming down my cheek?" Carter asked, keeping his voice steady. Still in shock, I didn't know how to answer him. "This tear coming down my cheek is my soul trying to escape this wretched body of mine to steal the love that you have discovered." After saying this he got up from his chair and went upstairs, leaving me at the dining room table. Now, although what Carter said to me was a bit dramatic, the dude was a self-educated man that read mostly Shakespeare plays and thick English novels from the eighteenth and nineteenth centuries. That's why he would express himself so deeply. I'm talking about a guy who would read us Sun

Tsu's *The Art of War* as part of our daily kung fu lessons. Shit, I couldn't catch him anywhere without a book in his hands.

As I left the dining room and made my way upstairs, I could hear the soulful sound of the Isley Brothers song, *Drifting on a Memory,* coming from Carter's room. Walking down the narrow hallway, I noticed that the door to his room was slightly ajar, and the light was on. With curiosity pushing me forward, I stood outside the door with one eye looking into the thin opening. That was when I saw Carter wrapping a blanket above his forearm tightly, causing a vein to bulge out and injecting it with heroin. His tears were now sliding down in thick streams, reminding me of a burst dam. It was at that moment that I saw a god crumble and destroy himself before my eyes.

With school starting up the following week and no sign of the girl from Camby Pool, I had decided to strictly focus on my training. Plus, I found that in some fucked up way my kung fu training with Carter helped to block out the image of him injecting heroin into himself. There wasn't a moment during our training when he looked like he was strung out. Shit, the dude was flawless during training, which made it easier for me to forget that he was using heroin. I never told anyone about Carter's addiction, not even Ace.

On the first day of school, me and Ace were standing outside the front doors to Alexis I. DuPont High School. Bored out of our minds and waiting for the doors to be unlocked, we started to talk shit about how the school year was going to turn out for us.

"Man, watch me holla at the flyest bitch in here," said Ace, transforming that statement into a high school boy's cliché. I smiled, trying to show interest in what Ace was saying, but I wasn't feeling it.

"Yo, what's your problem, nigga, you high or some shit?" Ace said, noticing that I was only half-listening.

"Nah man, just thinking about school is all."

Ace scrunched up his face, which let me know that he didn't believe a word I was saying. On the real, I was getting tired of Ace's immature ways and how he treated me. I know we were young back then, but that wasn't an excuse to go breaking hearts. Plus, I partly blamed him for possibly screwing up my chances with Chardy's homegirl.

"Man, I'm good, just thinking is all." I said, in the hopes that Ace would get off my back.

"Shit," Ace said, a hint of despair in his voice. I turned my head toward the direction he was looking and saw Chardey talking with the Spanish chick that stole my heart at Camby Pool a few weeks earlier. She was rocking a jet-black spandex suit with a zig zag royal blue line that ran down her right thigh. She also wore a washed-out jean jacket with a sewn-on Puerto Rico flag on one of the breast pockets. Letting my eyes roam the length of her body, l noticed that she had on a pair of black Rebok Classics to complete her look. Her large gold hoop earrings caught the light. Man…what caught my attention the most was her beautiful long brown hair cascading down her back. Such beauty was like a magnet, and I was drawn to it.

At that particular moment, I can't remember what Ace and I were talking about because I just left him talking by himself and made my way toward Chardey and her homegirl. Feeling the butterflies flutter in my stomach, my throat tightened. I feared that I wouldn't be able to talk, but to my surprise, I was able to say a soft "hello" before my nerves took over. Hearing my voice, both girls turned to face me. As soon as they saw me, though, their faces scrunched up into disgust, as if I was a piece of dog shit they had stumbled upon unexpectedly.

"Who the fuck said you could come over here?" asked Chardey's homegirl, seeming to remember that I was the homie of the dude that broke Chardey's heart.

"Chill ma, I just wanted to say what's up," I said casually.

Both girls rolled their eyes in unison and walked away. Chardey giggled and said to her, "Damn Sheila, that was harsh."

Chardey giggled. Both girls turned their backs on me, heading for the main entrance of the school.

On some real shit, though, I didn't feel disrespected. Nah, quite I felt quite the opposite. I felt happier than a mother-fucker 'cause I finally knew the Spanish broad's name. That entire day, the sound of her name rang throughout my head like a damn ear worm. My heart would beat wildly again my chest every time I would whisper to her. Ah, *Sheila*. The very thought of her made my knees weak.

Now, I know niggas will be like, "Man, that motherfucker Sammy is soft as shit. That pussy ass bitch ain't no gangster!" But to those that think that way, fuck 'em. On some real shit, we are all human and need love to sustain us. Unfortunately, though, shorty wasn't feeling the same way at the time. Although Sheila and I had most of our classes together, we didn't speak to one another because she would avoid me at all costs, all thanks to Ace's dumb ass. I knew I had to show her that I wasn't like Ace at all. I had to show her that I knew how to treat a lady, but how? At times, I would literally find myself talking to God, asking Him to please help me find a way that I could steal Sheila's heart. I would find myself crying my eyes out, asking God to help me find a way. As crazy as this might sound to nonbelievers, God did help me find a way to win Sheila's heart in the form of poetry.

In mid-November of that year, the English department of our school hosted a poetry slam. For those that wanted to sign up, they were directed to a sign-up sheet that was posted outside the cafeteria. One day, just out of curiosity, I looked over the names on the list. Lo and behold, I found Sheila's name. Taking out my pen from my back pocket, I quickly scribbled my name under hers and walked away. Coming home from school that afternoon, I ran up to my room and quickly began to write a poem, which went a little something like this:

> Her beautiful ancestry flows upon her flesh
>
> Like a majestic river, giving life to the Taino Indian queen
>
> That bathes in the pools of her eyes, cleansing her soul.
>
> If I look closely, I am able to appreciate the fine
>
> Architecture of the edifice that houses her soul:
>
> One that was fashioned by her great African.
>
> Ancestry, sculpting her hips and thighs.
>
> Just right.
>
> Meanwhile, she stands with the elegant grace of the queen of Spain.
>
> Oh, how l hunger to touch my lips to hers, making them pilgrims to
>
> A new land: a land so foreign to me, that touching it would result in my being destroyed only to be renewed in the essence of love.

The next day after school, my ass sat in a sweltering auditorium, listening to five or six suicide poems that all sounded the same. On the real, I was bored out of my fucking mind. Shit,

I was about ready to bounce without reading my poem, until Sheila's name was called. Man, she looked so sexy walking to the stage in her tight jeans, with Timberlands and a tight short sleeve T-shirt that didn't leave any room to the imagination. I can't say that I was all ears when she read her poem, but she definitely had my attention. Like I said before, her beauty was mesmerizing, and I was in a whole other world whenever she was around me.

After a few minutes of being in my little trance, the sound of my name being called shattered it and brought me back to reality. I got up from my seat with my back stiff and poem in hand. Making my way up the stage, I could honestly say that I didn't feel an ounce of nervousness. It was like one of those times where I had to prove myself during training with Carter. There was no room for chickening out.

I made my way up to the mic and said, "This poem is dedicated to Sheila Jade," and just did the damn thing. I was in the zone at that moment, and when I was done reciting my poem, I walked off the stage, pulling the hood from my sweatshirt on my head, and exited the auditorium.

In the hallway, making my way toward the exit of the back lobby, I was halted in my tracks by a girl calling my name. Turning around, I came face-to-face with Sheila.

"Did you really mean what you said in your poem?" she asked, hope shimmering in her eyes.

My heart was beating a mile a minute, and it took a second for me to respond. "Yeah, everything I said in that poem is what's in my heart," I said, trying to sound nonchalant about the matter. "I've been feeling you ever since that day I first saw you at Camby's."

Her expression seemed to soften at my confession, as if I had penetrated an invisible shield.

"Well, I'm sorry I dogged you out, but I had to defend my girl. Ace was an asshole to her."

On the real, I didn't give a fuck what she thought about Ace. At least she was talking to me at the moment.

"Man, I feel you. Don't even worry about it. I know how Ace can be sometimes," I said, shaking my head, hoping that I didn't sound like one of those dudes that would say anything to get in a girl's pants, even if it meant throwing their best friend under the bus.

After an awkward pause, Sheila cleared her throat and said, "I wouldn't mind hanging out sometime." She looked bashfully down at her feet, her cheeks reddening a bit.

"Yeah, I'm down for whatever," I responded, a bit too overzealous. Reaching into her into her back pocket, she produced the paper she had written her poem on and a pencil, scribbling on it rapidly.

"Here's my number," she said, handing me the piece of paper. Sheila's phone number was written neatly, with smiley faces and hearts circling it.

"Call me, okay? Maybe we can chill on Saturday," said Sheila, walking back toward the auditorium.

"I'll see you around," I said, watching her hips sway back and forth.

In the weeks that followed, Sheila and I were inseparable. Of course, I soon discovered that Sheila wasn't stuck up like Ace thought. As a matter of fact, she was exactly the opposite. This might have been because I was biased at the time, but Sheila was the most down-to-earth broad I have ever seen in my life. I never heard her bad mouthing or beefing with other chicks, and I never saw her fronting whenever we were together, despite there always being cats from school around. She was always herself, a genuine heart. I also found out that she was a huge anime nut. I could sit and watch her draw *Sailor Moon*,

Golgo 13, and *Speed Racer* for hours. We also would spend our time together walking around the whole Hilltop section of Wilmington, talking about our favorite poets and our favorite genre of music.

I could tell from the amount of time that we were spending together that she was feeling me as much as I was feeling her, so I kissed her smack dab on the lips, letting mine linger on hers for what seemed like eternity. When she didn't pull from me in disgust, I knew that she liked it. Releasing from our kiss, she put her head on my shoulder and whispered, "I love you, Sammy." As Sheila's words sunk into my heart, I could feel the cipher of my humanity solving itself.

Stepping out of that memory of Sheila and me and placing it back in the gallery of my mind, my thoughts returned to the present, in which I was lying next to Sheila as she slept. Kissing her forehead, I said a little prayer, thanking God for letting me be reunited with my queen. It was at that moment that I realized that was the first time I had spoken to God in twenty-seven years. Ironically, the two conversations I had with God came full circle, both having to do with Sheila. "I will burn in hell before I let anything happen to you," I vowed in a low whisper, barely audible as I kissed her forehead once again.

CHAPTER FIVE

I N THE WEEKS FOLLOWING MY RELEASE, I TRIED TO KEEP my nose clean, but for motherfuckers like me it is virtually impossible to stay out of trouble. Lord knows that I tried going the straight and narrow path, but once a nigga gets a taste of the streets, it's very hard to let that shit go. Don't get me wrong, the first week I was out of prison I got a regular nine-to-five job. Mami Yadi was nice enough to get me hooked up with one, working at a Dominican bodega on Fourth St. across from the old Latin American Community Center. But I just wasn't feeling it. Man, what I look like working as a damn stock boy at some bodega? Shit, I was a millionaire when I was working with the Zepedas crew. Now look at me, with a kelly green apron on and stocking fucking mangos.

Sheila would notice my disappointment when I would come home from work and say, "Cheer up, *Papi,* that book is gonna sell, and then you don't have to work at that bodega anymore."

The funny thing was, I completely forgot that she was done typing my book and had sent it off to a bunch of publishers, who had swiftly rejected it.

"Ma, ain't nobody gonna publish my shit, it's too hood," I said, raising my voice in frustration.

"Oh, I know you ain't talking to me like that, nigga," she retorted, turning from her position at the kitchen sink and getting up in my face. "Your ass ain't the only one adjusting to this new change. You gotta realize that even though my love for you never wavered in the past twenty-two years, I have to get used to the fact of physically having you here with me. Hell, there are times I wake up and the shit is scared out of me, because I am not used to having you by my side late at night. Or the times when you come home from work early, and you come up from behind me in your tippy toes and kiss me on the neck. That frightens me to death because I'm not expecting you. But you don't see me getting rowdy with you. That's just something I have to work through, so please don't make this transition hard on me."

I stood in the middle of the kitchen for a couple seconds, letting her words sink in. I ain't gonna lie, Sheila's words were like daggers to my heart, but she was being real with me. I had to respect that. I was at a loss for words at the moment, so I went to the front porch to sit on a rickety old lawn chair to smoke a blunt. If there was one thing that I hated the most about the ghetto, it's the fact that you can't see the stars at night because of the damn streetlights. So, I sat back with my blunt hand, envisioning the stars, which may see us humans as imperfect gods crumbling in the wind.

As these thoughts flowed through my mind, I failed to notice Ace walking up to my porch. I only became aware when I realized that a shadow was looming over me, blocking the faint orange glow from the streetlight that stood in my direction.

"What up nigga? Long time no fucking see," Ace said. At first, my brain couldn't register that it was his voice. Shit, that must have been some good ass weed for that to happen.

"Yo, wake up, nigga!" Getting annoyed with the damn shadow barking orders at me, I looked up at its face and realized that it was Ace.

"Oh, shit my dude, what's happening?!" I yelled excitedly, getting up from my chair to embrace my brother. I hadn't seen Ace in a minute. Last time I saw him was at Carter's funeral in 1994. After Carter's death, Ace and I went our separate ways. I stayed with the Zepedas crew while Ace did his shit with the drug game down in Miami, which I heard made him rich beyond his wildest dreams. *So, what was he doing back here in Delaware?* I wondered.

We broke from our brotherly embrace and sat down, Ace taking the lawn chair beside me, all cool and nonchalant in his white Sixers jersey with the fitted cap to match. "I heard you was doing life, nigga," said Ace.

"Yeah, that's true man, but I beat the case off some crazy ass loophole in the legal system that my lawyer found," I replied, taking a puff from my blunt.

"Shit, that must have been a hell of a lawyer to have found that loophole, 'cause your ass was buried. I mean it seemed that the only you were getting out of prison was via body bag," Ace said in a mock Jamaican accent as he reached for my blunt. "Aye man, don't be stingy, pass the Dutchie on the left-hand side."

I smiled, passing him the blunt. "Shit, for a while there I thought that I was going to die in that hell hole, but Sheila fired my old lawyer and got me this young cat by the name of Donald Goldman. I swear, nigga is a fucking genius," I said, conviction ringing in my voice.

Releasing thick clouds of marijuana smoke both from his mouth and nostrils, Ace looked like a humanoid dragon getting ready to breathe fire on an unsuspecting village, which brought a smirk to my face.

"Nigga, what're you smiling for?" asked Ace suspiciously.

"Did you know your ass always looks like some kind of weird dragon whenever you smoke?" I teased.

Ace gave me the side eye and said, "Nigga, I think you smoking something else besides the weed in this blunt. Anyway, nigga, I ain't come here to chit chat like two old ladies."

Ace took another puff from the blunt then continued.

"I came out here to ask you a favor," he said, looking me dead in the eye. It was then that I felt the darkness awaken within me, shaking itself off from a deep twenty-two-year-old slumber. I could feel it sitting up and licking its chops, awaiting its time to feed. Mind you, I would only feel this darkness awakening in me when it was time for me to kill. It was like a strange craving I couldn't control. I had to satisfy it immediately or go insane. Oddly enough, however, Ace asking me for a favor was the thing my darkness needed to awaken, and it was damned happy to be awake. You see, when Ace got right down to the point in a conversation, that usually meant that heads were going to roll, and blood was going to flood the motherfucking streets. Don't get it twisted: when I got out of prison, I vowed to walk a straight and narrow path, but when shit pops off and my brother Ace needs me, I am down for whatever the cause. Family over everything. That's what Carter taught us.

The front porch grew thick with silence. a heavy Afghan quilt that was suddenly draped over us. It wasn't hard to tell that Ace was choosing his words carefully before he spoke. I could figuratively see when his mind chose what he was going to say. On the real, the dude's face indicated that what he was going to tell pained him.

"We gotta take Zepedas out, nigga!" Ace blurted that shit out so quickly that I hardly understood what he had said. He must have seen the confused look on my face because he repeated what he said more clearly. "This ain't no joke, man. That fucking fat bastard is trying to muscle in on my coke and heroin business down in Florida, and a nigga ain't having that, you feel me?"

I sat there listening, confused as shit, trying to piece it all together. "Wait, I always thought that Zepedas been had Miami on lock."

"Damn nigga, I didn't know you was that far out the game!" Ace said angrily, as if I should have known better, then released a sigh of disappointment. "Back in the early 2000s, me and that fat fuck Zepedas had an agreement. We had both agreed that anything south of Miami was my turf, and anything north of Miami was his, including the whole East Coast of the United States. Nah, but nigga had to be greedy. He sent his niggas up to my most lucrative trap houses, killed a ton of my soldiers, and made off with at least a hundred thousand dollars. That motherfucker gotta get dealt with."

I couldn't believe what I was hearing. Shit, back in the day, Zepedas was nothing but good to us. That dude made us both millionaires, so you can imagine why I had to give my man the side eye.

"Dude, are you sure about this?" I asked skeptically, still trying to grasp what Ace was saying.

"Nigga, what I look like coming at you with a lie like that for? It's even an insult that you would ask me some stupid shit like that. As a matter of fact, peep this out, nigga," he continued, adding renewed vigor to what he was saying. "Zepedas is behind the reason you was locked up all them years. The cops was putting pressure on about the drugs he was selling because they want some more of his hush money. So, when the fat bastard said no, that's when the cops threatened to raid all of his stash house, which include putting word to the FBI about his dealings in other states. So, what did the nigga do?

He had your ass set up by Rico Red, except that Rico dying wasn't part of the plan."

I was taken aback by this revelation. I couldn't believe what I just heard. I didn't want to believe it, as a matter of fact.

"Yo, who gave you information?" I asked angrily.

Now it was Ace's turn to be shocked. "Nigga, what are you talking about? Everybody knows about that shit. Fuck, I'm surprised that you didn't find that out in the clink."

As Ace was telling me all of this, my mind started to crank out memories of my time in prison that I kept buried deep down the dark recesses of my subconscious; it brought out the haggard features of a fellow prisoner that had been severely scarred on his face. The scary thing was that the scars on this dude's face were arranged in weird shapes, as if a small child had done them. One of the scars on the man's face resembled a smiley face that was on his left cheek in the form of a crude jagged circle with a pair of eyes and a mouth that resembled a half-moon. The dude even the shape of tucking stick figures on his face that seem to dance every time he would say to me, "Zepedas set you up, man!"

I ain't pay him no mind, though, because I thought that the guy was a nut, with his Neo-Nazi tattoo on his forehead and his shaved head gleaming in the prison lights. The guy would constantly approach me every chance he got and repeat his claim about Zepedas. He would do this every day until he was found dead in an unused stairwell, with a shiv sticking out of the left side of his neck. Looking back at it now, in connection to what Ace had revealed to me, it seemed that someone wanted to silence the dude before he said too much.

With this thought eating away at my mind like strong acid eating through metal, I was now fully convinced that Zepedas and his crew needed to be taken out. Fuck living a normal life, this was personal. That fat fuck kept me away from Sheila for twenty-two years, and from my whole life. It was because of him that I never had the chance to start a family with Sheila in our younger years. To top the shit off, she was pregnant when I was arrested. The stress of my situation caused her to have a miscarriage. Yo, word on everything, that piece of shit was going down.

"I'm in, dog," I said, without giving it any more thought. My response activated a noticeable sense of confidence in Ace. It was as though a thousand pounds were lifted from his shoulders.

"I knew I could count on you, man," he said, giving me dap. "Meet me at Silverbrook Cemetery tomorrow at eight in the morning, by Carter's gravesite." He got up from his chair and headed down the porch steps.

"It was nice seeing you," he called out, without looking back at me, and headed toward the direction of St. Paul School. As he walked under a streetlight, I noticed that it flickered a faint orange glow and abruptly went out, leaving Ace to look like a dark, featureless silhouette roaming the night.

CHAPTER SIX

SITTING THERE ON THE PORCH, MY MIND WAS AT WAR with itself. Every fiber of my being wanted to go after Zepedas in full force, but I also had to think about the consequences going after an individual like him would entail. Attacking his entire organization meant that his associates would come after us, guns blazing, which meant cutting a deal with them ahead of time, letting them know what was going to happen to Zepedas's organization and then trying to get those associates on our side. That was going to be the hardest shit we had to do. That was my biggest concern about the situation. Shit, Zepedas had connections with all types of Mafia fighters all over the country, including both Jewish and Yakuza connections.

"What the fuck did I get myself into?" I asked aloud to the cool autumn night that was encompassing me.

Getting up from the lounge chair and entering the house, a dark force grabbed hold on my mind. It was as if my past as a hit man wanted to remind me of something; its cold fingers wrapping itself around my mind were pulling me toward a memory that I had thought lay buried in my unconscious.

Sheila cried alone with her back against her locker, our usual meeting spot when we skipped study hall. Making my way toward her, she kept turning her head in the opposite direction, trying to avoid looking at me.

"What's up with you, ma?" I asked, taken completely off guard by the way she was acting toward me. It was as though she was a timid puppy that didn't want to be touched by anyone. I placed my hand on Sheila to guide her toward me, causing her to jolt in fright, as if my very touch had stung her severely. I could feel the sky falling on me at that point. Sheila was never afraid of me; I had never given her reason to be. I gently moved her head toward me so I could look directly into her eyes. That was when I noticed that she had a black eye, along with what seemed like a sea of blood in the white of her right eye, which meant that one of her blood vessels in her eye had burst.

"What the hell happened to your eye, ma?" I asked, rage coursing through my veins. With fear in her eyes, she told me everything. It was like witnessing a dam bursting open.

"I got into a fight with my dad," she said in between sobs. "He told me to stop seeing you, and when I refused, he beat me."

As the last of her words left her mouth and sunk into my heart, I punched the locker beside her. It left a huge dent on its door that caused a loud clang, which echoed throughout the halls like a metallic groan of pain. It wasn't news to me that Sheila's pops didn't want me to see her. The motherfucker hated my guts. You would think that her pops was just being your run-of-the-mill, overprotective father, but there was something much sinister about their relationship. It was by those lockers that she confessed to me that her pops was raping her on a nightly basis. The rage coursing through my veins had reached its boiling point. I decided to take matters into my own hands.

"Sheila, everything is going to be alright, I promise," I said to her in a soft voice, trying to get my rage under control. I knew what to do then. It was time to get vengeance for Sheila, and I would call upon Ace for his assistance in the matter.

"Everything's going to be okay, baby," I repeated.

A few hours later, I caught up with Ace and told him all that went down with Sheila and her pops.

"Oh yeah, I know that nigga. He chills at the whore house down on route thirteen. Nigga be frontin' like a motherfucker, too. He's always telling the girls that he got mad stack when everybody knows that he's fucking broke, but the bitches like to humor him," said Ace, letting out a little chuckle as he puffed on a blunt. He knew that information about her pops because he was working for Zepedas as security at the whore house, which by all intents and purposes, should have been illegal as fuck. Ace was fourteen at the time, but physically he resembled a twenty-four-year-old body builder. He had the law in his pocket and could do whatever he pleased.

"Dude, that's perfect. I could wet him up right there on the spot. You think Zepedas will get salty if we use his spot to body that piece of shit?" I said, frustration oozing out of every fiber of my being.

Ace snorted in amusement at my question and said, "Fuck no, that fat bastard would be happy as hell if you got rid of Sheila's pops. That nigga owes him like a million dollars that we all know he ain't gonna pay back. Shit, you'll be doing the boss a favor. Matter of fact, I'll take you to go see Zepedas at one of his joints so that you can tell him about your situation."

So, it was settled. Ace set up a time and place where we were to meet Zepedas the next day.

Skipping school the next day, Ace and I set out to meet with Zepedas at one of his businesses: a rundown laundromat on Maryland Avenue that sat in the middle of a shopping mall, forgotten by time. Most of its stores had gone out of business since the late 1970s, and what remained were little mom and pop shops that were barely staying afloat.

Entering the laundromat, the smell of Clorox and other liquid detergents assaulted my nose, causing my breath to hitch. On the real, if I hadn't that, I would have thrown up all over my damn self.

"Just act cool, nigga. Stop acting like you scared or some shit. Wipe that worried look off your face too. The dude can smell fear, and believe me, if he does your ass will be invisible to him. It will be like you never even existed, so man the fuck up, nigga!" Ace said as we sat on a couple of metal folding chairs situated in front of a picture window facing the parking lot of the shopping center.

We sat in silence for what seemed like an eternity, watching the diverse clientele of the laundromat go through the motions of the mundane task of washing clothes. It was as though every individual in that place was a part of a fine-tuned machine that kept the laundromat alive. Every once in a while, the occasional crackhead would come up to where we were sitting and ask if we had any spare change, but Ace would quickly shoo them away, as if he were a dog owner who was fed up with his pet's shenanigans.

We had been waiting so long there that I began to observe a woman, battered and beaten by time itself. Her face was so sallow and wizened that it resembled dried up river beds. Her body was paper thin without a single curve in sight, making her white tube top and baby blue short shorts hang loose on her body. She looked like a human scarecrow. On the real, the bitch was fucking freaky looking, especially her eyes, which seemed sunken deep into her skull. Shit, it was no wonder that when she spoke to us, I almost jumped out of my skin.

"Hello, is anyone there?" the woman asked sarcastically. She rolled her eyes. "Are y'all fucking deaf? I *said*, the boss will see you now!"

Slowly getting up from our seats, we followed her to a back room behind a dirty whitewashed door. Placing her hand on the doorknob, she quickly turned around and yelled, "Tony, could you get these people the fuck out of here?!" referring to the laundromat customers.

"Will do, Lissey," the man at the counter said, getting up from his stool and shooing people out the front door.

"You Sammy?" Lissey asked, looking me directly in the face.

I nodded with an impassive look on my face, which caused her to smirk.

She shook her head and said, "So young and you're willing to take a life for the girl you love. Now that's a real man in my opinion." I could have sworn after she said that a tear was getting ready to slide down her left cheek, but she quickly turned her head toward the doorway so as not to let us see her emotion.

Entering the door was like entering the mouth of a demonic beast. My face was quickly assaulted by stank warm air, as if the room itself was breathing. The rhythmic hum of an old boiler made the room pulsate, as though it had an old heart on its last few beats. At that moment I could feel the gripping of my heart, as my eyes began to adjust to the darkness of the room. In front of us was a cinder block wall in desperate need of a paint job. The years of dust accumulating on the wall resembled the soot-stained face of a firefighter that just exited a burning building.

"Yo, Lissey, hurry the fuck up and bring those damn kids over here," a watery voice drenched in phlegm growled. Without responding to the voice that commanded her, Lissey walked around the corner from the entrance with Ace and me following her every step. Rounding the corner of the room, we found Sheila's pops tied to a chair. The man's wrists were bounded tightly behind him with dirty yellow rope digging into his flesh. His face was slick with sweat, anxiety clearly taking over his body. The motherfucker knew that he was going to die, and there was no escaping it. His mouth had been duct taped to muffle his screams during the preparation for this moment. I could hear the piece of shit beg for his life as I looked into his eyes. Those eyes pleaded volumes of forgiveness, but it was too late. He had hurt my love dearly and had to pay.

Under the naked lightbulb in the room, I saw an overweight man with thick gold rope chains around his neck and multiple tattoos on both of his arms. One of those tattoos was of a map of the island of Puerto Rico, with fine cursive writing that read *Mi Isla Bonita*.

"Hey, what the fuck, kid, you gonna kill him or are you just gonna stare at me and jerk off all day?" the overweight man growled, chilling my bones.

"Calm the fuck down, Zepedas, this is his first time doing this," Ace said, coming to my defense.

"Oh, I ain't realize that the little shit was a virgin to this type of thing. Let me tell you something, kid. When you want somebody dead, you kill them without having a second thought. You just say to yourself, *Hey, that piece of shit just fucked with my wellbeing,* then you kill the son of a bitch. Now, I know that you know this fact because you're Carter's boy and he trained you to be one of the most unstoppable killers on the face of the earth, but it seems to me that you're letting yourself get too caught up in your emotions over this punk ass's daughter to fulfill your duty at hand." Zepedas chuckled as he got up from his chair. The chain around his neck glistened in the light from the lightbulb, giving him a strange sort of dominant quality that screamed, *THIS CAT RUNS SHIT IN THE HOOD!*

Making his way toward me, I noticed that Zepedas was carrying a sledgehammer, its smooth jet-black head gleaming in the light, saying, *I'm ready when you are, little nigga.* Without saying anything else, Zepedas handed me the sledgehammer and backed away. But before I killed the bastard, I needed to hear why he hurt Sheila. Ripping the duct tape off his mouth, I felt glee when he winced in pain.

"Why are you doing this, Sam? I've been nothing but nice to you," Sheila's pops said, playing the innocent, oblivious victim. I could feel the anger start to course through my body. I took a deep breath before answering. Drool dripped from the sides of my mouth, as if I was a rabid dog. "You raped her, Julio!" I screamed, my spit raining down on his face.

As if disregarding the fact that he was going to die, Julio let out a torrent of laughter and said, "Aww, *pobrecito,* I thought you knew she was a little whore."

At this point it seemed that he no longer gave a fuck what happened to him. He was just trying to fuck with my emotions for as long as he could.

"Yeah, little man, I done popped that bitch's cherry when she was twelve and she liked it, begging for me to—" Cutting him off mid-sentence, I swung the sledgehammer as hard as I could, sending the bastard's head clean off his body and smacking into the wall on the left side of the room.

"Holy shit, did you see that?! Little dude just went Babe Ruth on that *cabron,*" said Zepedas more to himself than to the people in the room. Zepedas was so impressed that he instantly dubbed me "El Demonio," or *The Devil* in Spanish. Aside from giving me that moniker, it was that day that he put me on about being a full-time enforcer for his crew. I can still hear Ace's voice that day as it echoed throughout the streets on our way home.

"You owe me, nigga!" Ace kept saying, jumping up and down with excitement. "Yo, do you realize that you are now part of the biggest and baddest crew in Delaware? This is fucking major, baby."

Making my way up to my room, I found Carter sitting by my window and looking out onto the backyard, which was nothing but concrete and a few dead plants. I didn't say a word and just stood there at the doorway to my room observing Carter's emaciated form. Heroin had taken its toll on his once robust physique, turning him into a frail old man at age forty-five.

"I know what you did today, Sam," he said, as he kept staring out the window. "I talked to Zepedas a few minutes ago over the phone. He said that you are a little wet behind the ears, but you're a cold-blooded killer, didn't even flinch when you saw that guy's head flying across the room."

It was at that moment that Carter stopped talking and I lost all my composure. Tears began to flow down my face, as I held out my arms for an embrace. Not once in my life did Carter hug me, but that day, he hugged me as though he was trying to keep me from withering away in the wind.

"It's okay to cry, Sam. It means that you have a heart and you're still human. Shit, if you didn't cry after your first murder, I would be worried, but that just means that your heart isn't cold. Do you understand what I'm saying?"

He broke our embrace. That was the first and only time he hugged me. It was then that I knew he loved me like a son. Two weeks later, Ace and I found him dead in bed with a needle stuck in his arm. He had overdosed the night before.

"One love, pops," I said, as the memory of my first kill and Carter's death relinquished its hold on me, allowing me to return to the late fall of 2017.

CHAPTER SEVEN

"**B**ABE, BABE WAKE UP, YOU GOTTA COME SEE THIS," said Sheila. Seeing that I wasn't waking up quick enough, she resorted to hitting me over the head with a pillow. "Babe, wake the fuck up, I got good news!" she said, adding more excitement to her already hyped voice. Wiping the crust away from my eyes, I planted my feet firmly on the floor. Without a word, Sheila handed me a print copy of an email she had received from a publishing company, called Hood Renaissance.

According to the email, the company had received my manuscript and had decided to take it on. I couldn't hold back my excitement and happiness. Lifting Sheila off her feet, both of our bodies spun around the room in extreme bliss.

"I have some more good news to tell you, said Sheila, her eyes gleaming with a certain kind of happiness and freedom that I had not seen since the day I got rid of her pops.

"What is it?" I asked, feeling overwhelmed.

Tears slid down her cheeks as she said, "I'm pregnant, babe."

Overjoyed with this announcement, I kissed her passionately on the lips, but our little moment was interrupted by the ringing of the house phone. I quickly broke away from Sheila's embrace and headed toward the phone, because all my instincts told me it was Ace who was calling.

"Nigga, is that you?" His words rushed out, sounding irritated.

"Well, hello to you too," I said sarcastically, hoping to lighten Ace up a bit.

"Look man, we gotta take out Zepedas and his crew now. They're all at a poker game as we speak. We can hit them all now with one swoop and we're done, you feel me?"

Ace's logic seemed reckless to me, going into a poker game full of gangsters and shooting them up with no plan whatsoever. However, I was sure Ace knew what he was doing, so I was down.

"Yo, I'm outside right now in my car with Uzis in the trunk and a shit load of ammo. It's now or never," said Ace, hanging up the phone.

I ran out the front door without saying anything to Sheila, not even looking back to see the expression on her face. I saw Ace behind the wheel of a beat-up old Lincoln. I opened the passenger door and hopped in. Ace was dressed in a black jumpsuit that made him look like he was going to an audition for the role of Michael Myers in the next *Halloween* flick, complete with white mask and all, which was on his lap as he drove. It didn't take long for me to figure out that he had the same getup for me to wear as well. Without saying a word, I put on the jumpsuit as he drove and placed my Uzi in my lap.

When we made it to the poker game, held in an old first floor apartment near Orange Street, we put on our masks, grabbed our guns, and exited the car, making our way inside the apartment building at full speed like Navy SEALs. Entering the building, we kicked in the door to apartment 1A, letting our Uzis spit round after round at group of men sitting around a poker table. Things were going so fast that I didn't even see the dude's faces, but the one face that I saw and was familiar with was that of Zepedas's, now lying dead on the floor.

As we ran back to our car, a sudden thunderous crack of a shotgun sounded behind us, leaving Ace's head in a bloody pulpy mess. I made all the way to the driver side door of the Lincoln when I felt a bullet rip through the left side of my torso. On the real, I thought that was all she wrote for me, but I knew it wasn't my time. I could feel it in my heart.

Believing I wasn't going to die, my thoughts quickly gathered themselves into an energy I hadn't felt since I was a teenager, an energy I only felt during my training with Carter. This energy encompassed my soul, causing me to react as a man possessed. It was as though the shotgun blast that knocked me out awakened something that had been dormant in me for years, something that spoke to me in Carter's voice. It was like I was in the middle of one of our training sessions.

"Get up, nigga! That shotgun blast just grazed you. Move your ass, nigga," Carter's voice yelled in my mind, causing me to shrug off the daze that I was in and forcing me to open my eyes to see my would-be killer standing over me as if he was a predator out in the wild examining his prey. The piece of shit must have had something on his mind distracting him, because he didn't notice when I picked my Uzi and fired a few shots into his face. He fell to the pavement awkwardly with his arms flailing like a strange bird.

"Now's your chance nigga. Move!" said the voice in my head. Getting up from the pavement, I could see a huge crowd gathered across the street, gawking at me with their mouths hanging open. It was as though they were witnessing a dead man rising from the grave. At the same time, I could hear the wailing sirens approaching us on Orange Street. With all the strength that I could muster, I limped into the driver seat of the Lincoln and found a spare key hidden in the visor above. After starting the ignition, I quickly fishtailed the car onto the road, making tires screech like a banshee escaping the depths of hell as I sped away from the scene.

My mind kept racing with jumbled thoughts. My mind kept going back to Ace, lying dead on the pavement with his head blown off. *What the fuck am I going to do now?* At that moment it was obvious that the Zepedas family already knew Ace and I were behind that whole fiasco. No doubt they also knew that I was still alive. Despair suddenly took over me. I felt like a chicken with its damn head cut off, completely lost at that point.

"Man the fuck up, nigga!" Carter's voice yelled in my head. "Your main priority right now is to get Sheila and get the fuck up out of dodge. I know you're mourning Ace and want to retaliate, but you need to forget about all that shit and focus on your family right now. Get out of this street life while you still can and forget about seeking vengeance. It's not worth it. Just look at how Ace ended up."

I guess my body was on autopilot, because as soon as Carter's voice ceased, I found myself parked in front of my home but having no recollection whatsoever of the desire to head over there. I swear, my mind completely blacked out as soon as I got in the Lincoln and drove off from the scene at Orange Street.

I jumped out of the car and ran to the porch. Placing my hand on the knob, my heart sank as I found the door unlocked. Sheila never left the front door unlocked. It was one of her pet peeves. Something was definitely wrong. Opening the door with the force of a hurricane wind, I ran inside like a madman, screaming Sheila's name at the top of my lungs, only to be greeted with the scene of a huge struggle. The glass coffee table that sat in the middle of the living room now was shattered into a million pieces. The cream-colored sofa was overturned, along with the end tables and two busted lamps.

"Sheilaaaa!" I yelled at the top of my lungs. I searched throughout the house for her with no success. Making my way to the dining room, I discovered a handwritten letter on the dinner table. It read:

Hello there Sammy,

Why the fuck did you think that you and Ace could pull a fast one on me? I didn't realize that you motherfuckers were so stupid. Jesus, I thought Carter taught you two better than that? Weren't you two trained in the art of Ninjitsu or some shit like that? If so, then y'all motherfuckers are terrible at it! Anyway, all jokes aside, we've been watching your ass since you got out of prison, so we knew every move you made. For a while you played the part of a good boy, but you let Ace convince you to fight against us. That was one of your biggest mistakes. You knew as well as I did that Ace was a fucking hothead, so why did you join him on his fool's quest? Come on Sam, anybody in these streets will tell you that there ain't no loyalty out here, it's every man for himself. That is why I have taken your wife, to toughen you up. Little bitch! Until we meet again.

Tony Zepedas

CHAPTER EIGHT

MY ENTIRE WORLD SEEMED TO CRUMBLE ALL AROUND me at that moment. Tony Zepedas? I thought that little shit had died years ago. As a matter of fact, I was the one that did the deed. Tony Zepedas was the only son of the head of the Zepedas family. His pops had me take the kid out because he was causing some major beef with the Haitians down in Miami, when he wanted to team up with a small Cuban and Puerto Rican crew without his pops knowing anything about it. However, it was by way of the Haitians that his pops found out, after a couple dudes from the crew that Tony wanted to do business with snubbed them out. That's when old man Zepedas called me in to kill his son.

I remember that shit like it was yesterday. I had been spying on the bastard all week, waiting to see if he made any moves that would do any harm to his pops' business. Tony met with a rival Puerto Rican crew that established themselves in an old rundown bodega on Franklin Street. They were nothing, though, just a couple of former stickup kids looking to rise up in the ranks. Aside from that, the dude was pretty boring. When he wasn't chilling with his little bodega crew, he would stay indoors in his Greenville townhouse, having high price hookers come over. At night, Tony could be found in the manager's office in a strip club owned by his pops, called The

King's Lounge. It was there that I decided to make my move. That night I had followed him to the club's basement.

As planned by my boss, the cellar doors were left unlocked, granting me easy access without being noticed. Making my way to the office, I could hear Vanity 6's "Nasty Girls" blasting throughout the club. Nobody noticed me going up the stairs to the manager's office. They were all entranced by the thick White girl dancing topless onstage.

At the top of the stairs, I kicked the door open, interrupting one of the strippers giving head to Tony. She looked up at me like a deer caught in headlights, and before she could scream, I pulled out my silencer and gave Tony two shots to the dome, splattering his brains all over the wall. For good measure, I shot the stripper he was with between the eyes, in case she got any bright ideas to start screaming for help. The hit went off without a hitch, or so I thought, and I left the club to report back to the boss.

Now, twenty years later, I stood in my kitchen with a note that felt like it had been written by a ghost. Pondering this notion, I felt a sudden movement behind me, causing me to elbow then roundhouse kick whatever was behind me. When I felt that it was safe to let my guard down, I saw a dude dressed in black with a ski mask, squirming in pain on the kitchen floor. Out of the corner of my eye, I saw the handgun that my attacker used lying a few feet away from him, and I quickly snatched it up. Pointing the gun at my attacker, I realized that his skills were nowhere near that of a trained assassin, so I relaxed my guard a bit.

"Who sent you?" I asked, kicking the motherfucker in the ribs. Despite the pain he was feeling, the bastard didn't answer my question, so I kicked him again, this time hearing his ribs crack painfully.

"Tony sent me!" he screamed in submission. I leaned over him this time and yanked off his ski mask. I wanted to see his face when I asked him my next question, but what was revealed behind that mask was the face of a young boy, who couldn't have been no more than sixteen.

"You little shit, how you gonna roll up in my house and try to kill me? Do you know who the fuck you're dealing with, faggot?" I asked the boy. His eyes began to overflow with the fear inside of him. It was at that moment that I could feel the darkness that I had repressed for twenty-two years come back full force. Carter's voice echoed in my mind, saying, *"Welcome back, nigga!"*

With that giving me the strength that I needed, I struck the boy in the face with a gun, causing the boy to bleed from his lower lip.

I grabbed the boy by his head, pulled his face up to mine and screamed, "Where the fuck is my wife?!"

My voice sounded ferocious, like that of a wild animal. The boy stammered, piss forming in a puddle around him. "Sh-sh-she's in a a wa-wa- warehouse in Philly," he finally spat out.

Thanks," I said, putting the barrel of the gun underneath his chin and blasting the little fucker's brains out.

CHAPTER NINE

IT WASN'T HARD FOR ME TO FIGURE OUT WHICH WARE-house the kid was talking about. If there was one thing about the Zepedas family, they were creatures of habit. If they established themselves in a place and a rival family tried to attack, the Zepedas family would find a way to eliminate them and continue business as usual in the same spot. Sure, it was very high risk to operate in such fashion, but they were very arrogant folk. Those motherfuckers felt that they couldn't be touched. However, they didn't seem to take into account that they would go up against a dude like me who knew how they operated, and I knew damn well that Tony knew this fact and had big plans for when we met face-to-face. But I had something up my sleeve. I was going to take down all the major Zepedas operations one by one before I saved Sheila, and if Tony was watching me like he said was, I welcomed his goons to come at me.

As I thought this through, the adrenaline in my started to subside, and I felt the pain on the side of my body where the shotgun slug had grazed me earlier in the day. Getting some thread and sewing needle from a cabinet upstairs, I headed to the bathroom to clean and sew up my wound, using a hand mirror to view my handiwork.

That night, I drove Ace's Lincoln out to Eastside and abandoned it on the side of the road. Exiting the car, I walked to the trunk and banged on it, saying, "Happy trails to you, motherfucker!" Laughing out loud, I thought of my attacker, whose corpse was lying stiff and curled up in the trunk. I could feel a little drop of remorse begin to seep into the barricade of darkness that housed my soul once again, as if it was a leaky roof during a heavy rainstorm. But that weak spot was quickly patched up. *The kid asked for it.* Shit, I was defending myself. The piece of shit came at me first. Then I thought of Ace. *How did he know that old man Zepedas and the main dude that helped run his businesses were going to be at that exact apartment playing poker?*

It was then that a lightbulb went off in my head. Right then and there, it became obvious to me that Ace had some kind of dealings with Tony. My blood began to boil with rage. Ace might have hidden the existence of Tony from me. Did Ace plan to fuck me over by teaming up with Tony to take out both his pops and me? Or maybe Tony was using us as pawns to wipe out his pops and his partners, and then kill us both after the job was done. I would like to think that the latter was true, and not that Ace wanted to set me up, but it was too difficult to say at that time. I didn't know if my thoughts were accurate, but I knew I would find out once I found Tony.

Night was fast approaching as I walked down the road. I was so preoccupied with my thoughts that I had completely forgotten that I was walking down a lonely road on the Eastside, putting myself at risk of getting robbed or jumped by a stickup kid or worse. I didn't give a fuck. I was on a warpath. After walking for three hours straight, I came across a small gun shop that had a sign out front that said, Welcome to Hank's! American-

Owned and Operated Since 1972. I could hear a southern twang punctuate the words as I read them.

"Ah, just what I need right now," I said to myself, bringing the preparation for my mission back into focus. As I walked into the gun shop, the first thing I saw was a huge Confederate flag hung up high on the wall with "This is God's Country" stitched on it. It was then that I knew I had entered a redneck's gun shop. Its walls were plastered with all kinds of posters that promoted the NRA. There was a wall strictly reserved for big game hunting trophies, which were the heads of bears and tigers. Their eyes stared back at me cold and blank.

"Can I help ya there, fella?" said the voice of an old man with a southern drawl. I nearly jumped out of my fucking skin when I heard that voice. I looked down from the big game trophies and saw an old White dude that was about seventy-nine years old, with a neon red baseball cap that read, Make America Great Again. Aside from the baseball cap, the dude had an extremely long, snow-white beard that went almost all the way down to his potbelly, making him look like some kind of a wizard. His plaid shirt and denim overalls smelled of tobacco and mold, as if the dude had been standing in the same spot behind the counter since the store had opened.

"What, are you deaf there, partner?" repeated the old man, attitude in his voice, snatching my attention from the big game trophies and bringing it back on him.

"Um, yeah, I'm looking for an AK-47 and bullets to go with it," I responded nonchalantly.

The old man gave a little chuckle at my request, but his eyes seemed to burn with the bigotry that he held inside. "That's it, just an AK47 and some bullets? You don't want a brand or model?" He shook his head sighing deeply. "It figures that a spic like you don't know a goddamn thing about no gun.

All you fuckers care about is killin' each other like those damn niggers."

I could feel my rage boiling. I closed my fist and punched the old fuck in the face, sending his head back with a grotesque crack, instantly killing him. With the sound of his body hitting the floor, I took that as my cue to help myself to all the shit that I needed. Seeing that I was the only one in the shop at the time, I quickly turned off the flashing sign that indicated the shop was open, and a few other lights.

Observing my surroundings, I noticed that the shop was packed with a ton of hunting clothes, everything from combat boots and hunting vests to a shitload of apparel that was strictly camouflage. Oddly enough, the place even sold long leather jackets, the ones that resembled trench coats. Immediately, I started to gather all the things needed for what lay ahead—a trench coat, as well as a Rambo-style hunting knife, an AK-47, and a ton of bullet clips. A nigga was ready for war. I wasn't playing. As that thought went through my mind, it dawned on me that there was most likely a security camera in the shop. I quickly scanned for some sort of room that a security system might be installed in. My eyes soon landed on a door behind the counter that read Employees Only.

"Jackpot," I said, jumping over the counter and breaking open the lock on the door. Inside, I saw what looked to be an old closed-circuit TV, with a VCR whizzing a VHS tape inside of it. The TV monitor displayed a black-and-white, top-down view of the shop. I quickly ejected the tape and stomped the shit out of it, destroying the damn thing as best I could. After disposing of the tape, it didn't take long for me to realize that the room that the room I was standing in housed a plethora of guns, grenades, and explosives.

"Fuck, I actually did this country a favor by killing that piece of shit, it looked like he was preparing for a war or some shit," I said out loud, remembering the Neo-Nazi fucks in prison jabbering on about how there was going to by a race war in America between Blacks and Whites. Well, I guess those White boys were now down one soldier.

Taking a few grenades and six bombs, shoving them in a large coach bag that I found in the shop, I walked out of the back door, which led out to a small garage that housed an old white van that had no side windows on its back half. The van itself reminded me of the kind that pedophiles used to kidnap kids.

"This must be my lucky day," I said, finding an extra set of keys to the van hanging from a peg by the door. Before I drove away in that ancient monstrosity, I needed to check it out first. Opening the van's rear doors, I discovered that there was an old army cot with a pillow and a thin blue sheet, provoking fatigue to take over my body. The toll of the day's events had finally affected me. I figured that with rest, I could better formulate a plan to take down the Zepedas family.

As soon as my body fell on that cot, I was out like a light. I dreamed of Sheila that night. That particular dream consisted of a memory of our first date. It had been two weeks after the poetry reading where I had gotten her attention. We had agreed to meet at Banning Park at dusk. Sheila had come equipped with a small AM/FM radio and a beach blanket with Bart Simpson embossed on it. It had a word bubble that read, "Don't Have a Cow, Man." We found a nice quiet spot on a grassy knoll where Sheila laid out her beach blanket and turned on her radio dial to Power 99 FM. As she messed with it, my eyes were glued to the sky. Dusk had now turned into night, allowing me to see a kingdom of stars for the first time in my life. On the real, it was so beautiful that I almost cried, but I was soon sidetracked by a romantic thought that I decided to share with Sheila.

"Yo, Sheila, you ever wonder if the stars confuse us for their gods?"

She looked over at me as a slight giggle escaped her mouth. "Nigga, do you ever turn that poetic shit off?" she asked jokingly, then kissed my lips. As if on cue, "Pretty Brown Eyes" by Mint Condition began to play softly on the radio. The soft sweet melody of the song had us in a trance, causing us to get up and slow dance.

"I love you, Sammy," whispered Sheila in my ear. That's when I pulled back to look into her eyes and discovered that her face had melted down to her skull. She screamed, "Wake the fuck up, nigga!" These words were said in a demonic voice, jolting me from my sleep.

Drenched in sweat and trying to catch my breath, a plan finally came to me. I was going to take down Zepedas in the city's four main trap houses, and the one he had down in Florida as well. Those four trap houses were the spine of the family's entire operation. Taking those houses out would cripple them for good. Those motherfuckers were surely going to feel my wrath. I could feel my blood boiling in anticipation as I got into the front seat of the van and headed to the first trap house on West Fourth Street.

Parking three blocks from my intended target, I donned the long leather coat that I nabbed from the gun shop, stuffing one of the small bombs in one of its inner pockets. I ain't gonna lie, the weight of the small bomb in my pocket made me feel like I was invincible. It was as though the bomb itself created a powerful force field around me that emanated pure death to anybody that tried to take my life. This feeling was so strong that instead of taking a gun with me, I chose the damn hunting knife. Exiting the van, I put my hood up over my head and started to walk like a junkie aching to get a fix. Dragging my feet along the pavement while scratching my arms, I could feel the cool breath of the dawn encompass my body. It was as though the darkness of predawn was clinging as a way to survive the oncoming daylight.

Passing the row homes on West Fourth, I could feel my old ways coming back to me, as if I was a demon was awakened from its slumber, ready to play. I could feel it flexing its muscles and getting its blood coursing through its numb limbs, ready to stalk and kill its prey.

Closer to the trap house, I noticed that one of Tony's lackeys was sitting on the front stoop with plastic white earbuds plugged into his ears, his eyes glazed over by a memory probably conjured up by whatever he was listening to. Hoping that the kid's distraction would buy some time to sneak up behind him and slit his throat, I hid in the shadows provided by a few parked cars beside the curb. Slowly taking out my hunting knife, I saw no need to pretend that I was a junkie when I could just sneak up behind the fucker and take him out. However, if this was back in the day, I would definitely have had to play the part of a junkie because the cats that Zepedas had working for him were like night owls, alert as shit. Hell, it didn't matter to none, I was right at home in the shadows, letting them embrace me like old friends at a welcome back party.

I stayed laid up against a parked car directly under a busted streetlamp, giving me the perfect cover as I waited for the piece of shit to turn his back against me so that I could make my move. With hands tucked into his dark Sean John coat, the dude got up from the stoop and turned to go in the house. Thanks to the music that blasted through his earbuds, I didn't have to conceal the sounds of my footsteps on the pavement, allowing me to move quicker.

Sneaking up behind the bastard, I slashed his throat without hesitation, his thick, dark blood cascading from the wound onto the front of his coat. The poor fuck didn't even know what hit him. Before the corpse could hit the ground, I hoisted it up over my shoulder like a sack of potatoes and carried him inside. The dude's earbuds had fallen out dangling at the sides of his face, granting me the chance to hear what he was listening to when I killed him.

"When I die bury me inside the Gucci store. All I want for my birthday is a big booty hoe!"

I ain't even gonna front, I felt like laughing my ass off when I heard the shit that cat was listening to when he died.

"Well, it looks like I did you a favor, kid. Shit, anybody who is a fan of shitty rap like that needs to be put out of their misery," I mumbled, putting the body down in a living room filled with crackheads and heroin addicts who were too high to care that I'd put a dead body among them.

The smell of piss, shit, and vomit assaulted my nose as I proceeded to the second floor of the house, tiptoeing up the stairs with my bloody knife in hand. The sound of Jodeci's hit song "Feenin'" floated softly down the stairs, which gave me the indication that there was at least one person on the second floor. This prompted me to be hypervigilant of my surroundings.

"Careful, nigga, there could be a motherfucker waiting to slit your throat at the top of those stairs," cautioned the voice of Carter in my head. At the top of the stairs, I have to say that I was slightly disappointed to discover that there was no one ready to attack me. Lord knows that my ass was prepared for anything at that point. Instead, when I made it to the landing on the second floor, I came upon a dimly lit hallway that smelled of blueberry-scented candles wafting from an open bedroom door where the sounds of Jodeci emanated from.

Pressing my body against the wall next to the open doorway, I could hear the passionate groans of a Spanish broad getting dicked-down.

"Aye, asi. Damelo duro, cabron!" the chick groaned in her Puerto Rican dialect.

Peeking into the room, I noticed that it was pitch black, save for a stream of light that streamed through the crack in the door. From what I could see, dude was pounding the broad's shit like there was no tomorrow. Seeing that the chick's eyes were closed, and her man's back was turned toward the door, I tip-toed in the room and slashed the dude's throat while he was in mid-hump. His body slid off the chick, falling sideways off the bed as he clutched his bloody throat, hopelessly trying to stop the massive hemorrhaging. The broad the dude was fucking let out a high-pitched scream when she realized what was going on, but that was no bother. I simply grabbed her by the face and rammed her head into the headboard with all my strength, hearing a satisfying crack as I crushed the back of her skull.

As I left the room, my attention was captured by the vibrating sound of a cell phone. Curious, I approached the nightstand and picked up the phone, reading the text message that was just left. "The hit on Don Goldman is a go for tonight. The bitch is already at his crib. That lawyer faggot is going to regret ever crossing us," it read. My heart dropped into my throat. *What kind of shit did Goldman have going on with the Zepedas crew?* I wondered. Whatever it may have been, I needed to warn his ass, pronto.

CHAPTER TEN

"*A*RE *YOU RETARDED, NIGGA? THAT DAMN FOOL IS AS GOOD as dead. Focus on your own shit!*" The voice of Carter was echoing wildly in my head as I ran down to the basement of the house. I duct taped the small bomb that was in my coat to a pillar. Luckily, I knew for a fact that this house in particular didn't have workers packaging the drugs in the basements of other homes, which meant it would be easier to set the bomb with no problem. Descending the creaky wooden steps, I saw stacks upon stacks of crack cocaine and heroin against a wall, almost as though the entire stack was a makeshift pillar holding up the house.

"Damn, all this product here and so carelessly guarded," I said out loud, in an attempt to block out Carter's voice from my mind. I guess that's the way things were with the Zepedas family. Hell, I ain't gonna front. If I was the head of a crew that monopolized the entire drug game in Delaware, I would be kind of careless too.

I set the bomb's timer to go off in five minutes and ran back up to the living room to see if I could steal a cell phone off one of the addicts that were stoned out their minds. Luckily, it only took a couple seconds to dig into an addict's pockets and come away with an old school flip phone. Exiting the house, I could honestly say that at that particular moment I felt no remorse for what happened to those addicts when the house blew up. Shit, as far as I was concerned, I was doing society a favor. They just happened to be in the wrong place at the wrong time.

The sun had risen as I walked back to the van. Jumping into the driver seat and closing the door, a monstrous boom sounded throughout the block and shook the ground beneath me. I couldn't help but smile as I drove away. People were running out of their homes, scared shitless over what they just heard and felt. Hell, some of those poor souls must have thought that the end of the world was upon them, or that some crazy dragon was wreaking havoc in the ghetto. Little did they know that it was just an old-ass Puerto Rican trying to save the life of his woman and getting his revenge.

So as not to hit the people that were running wildly in the street, I drove slowly, and dug into my pants' pocket. I took the flip phone that I had nabbed and dialed Goldman's number. To my relief, he picked up on the first ring.

"Who the fuck is this?!" yelled Goldman on his end of the phone, gasping for air. At that moment, I didn't care what the hell he was doing, I just wanted him out of harm's way.

"Listen to me, Donald," I said in a grim, serious tone without any type of greeting whatsoever. "I need you to listen to me very carefully, man. The Zepedas family has a hit put out on you."

On the real, when I broke that news to him, I thought his ass would have been shocked and scared shitless. Instead, Goldman sounded gangster about the whole thing.

"Yeah, no shit, man. I just iced my so-called assassin a few minutes ago."

At first, he was being sarcastic, but as soon as I realized he was trying to catch his breath without making some smartass joke, I knew he was serious. Without me asking Goldman for details of how everything went down, he began to give them rapidly, as if his mouth was a machine gun spitting round after round.

"Dude, I was fucking this fine Latin babe, and she was riding my dick like a good ole' cowgirl. Suddenly, while I'm all up in the pussy, the bitch decided to pull a knife out of nowhere. Luckily, my ass got quick reflexes, and I tagged her in the face, causing the bitch to fall to the floor. Seeing that she was dazed from the blow to the face that I'd just given her, I got on top of her with all my weight and started to bang her head on my hardwood floor until she stopped squirming, and her head was in a puddle of blood."

By the time Goldman finished his story, I could tell he was shaken. I sighed as I tried to figure out why Tony Zepedas would put a hit out on Goldman. *What has he gotten himself into?* I had to know the answer. Shit, that hit could have had something to do with me. Maybe Goldman knew something that l didn't.

I cleared my throat. "Where you at now, Donald?"

There was silence on the other end of the phone, showing me that there were trust issues floating around in Goldman's mind.

I let the silence draw out for at least two minutes before I said, "I'm trying to help you, Don. I am not working for Zepedas anymore. The piece of shit has been fucking me over for years. Anyway, Ismael Zepedas is dead now, but now his son Tony is in charge of the entire operation."

I could sense the relief in Goldman, as a deep sigh broke the silence on the other end of the phone. "Who killed the bastard?"

I couldn't help but sense the optimism in his voice. Confident that the phone I wasn't tapped by law enforcement or the Zepedas crew, I nonchalantly stated that I had killed Ismael.

There was a slight pause on the other end before Goldman answered. I could feel the tension growing as the minute of silence seemed to stretch out into eternity.

"You did what now?" The alarm in Goldman's voice flew into hysterics, as if he was on the edge of insanity. "Hold on, let's backtrack a bit," said Goldman, taking deep shallow breaths as if he was hyperventilating. "You killed Zepedas because he fucked you over?"

Judging from the tone of his voice, I could tell that he didn't believe me, causing me to sigh in frustration.

"Look man, where the hell are you?" I asked, letting it ride the wave of my annoyance.

"Alright, dude, chill," said Goldman with fear in his every word. "I'm holed up at Luck's Motel right off the Jersey turnpike."

I could sense a deep regret in his voice, which awoke suspicion right away. I knew right then that the motherfucker was planning to kill me.

I must have been out of my mind going to meet up with a dude that I thought was going to kill me, but I had to seek him out on the off chance that he was just scared and needed protection. Aside from that fact, I realized that I needed help on my mission. There was no way in hell I could take down Zepedas's empire on my own. Shit, not just with that bomb I set off in that trap house. At that very moment, I realized that the Zepedas family were doubling up on their manpower, and I was too fucking old for that one-man army Rambo shit. The way I saw it, maybe Goldman knew somebody that would be willing to help me out, that is, if I could prevent him from killing me first.

CHAPTER ELEVEN

Entering New Jersey, the first thing that caught my eye was a huge sign shaped like a giant domino piece, boldly displaying Lucky's in fancy letters like it was the name of some five-star hotel. Sadly, that wasn't the case. The building that the sign advertised was nothing more than a clapboard piece of shit. It only boasted eight rooms and a gravel parking lot with just two cars parked in it, Goldman's Benz and what I assumed to be the motel owner's navy-blue Ford pickup truck. The gravel in the parking lot crunched underneath the tires of the van, definitely alerting those inside the motel that someone had arrived. I figured that Goldman now knew that l was here, for sure. I could picture him next to a window standing behind a curtain yellowed with age, a semi-automatic rifle cocked like Malcolm X daring someone to attack.

Approaching Goldman's room at the end of the motel, I could sense that someone was following me, but I played it cool and went about my business. Jesus, Tony must have forgotten who he was messing with. I should have felt insulted, but instead felt elated at the fact that the predictability of Tony's crew would make it easier for me to kill. I just wished that I had been carrying a sniper rifle with me at that moment, so I could pick the fucker off that was following me without giving him a chance to attack. It would have been less messy in my opinion and a hell of a lot quicker too, but what's done was done.

I knocked on Goldman's hotel door, expecting him to open it right away with a gun pointed at me, but I was greeted with a set of muffled voices on the other side of the door. "See, I knew that lawyer bastard was gonna light you up, but you just had to come and save his ass. Nigga, did you ever pay attention to what I taught you? Now they're gonna light *your* dumbass up," scolded Carter.

I jumped out of the way of the sudden machine gun rounds piercing the door from inside. At that moment, shots also rang out from behind me. I took cover behind a pillar holding up an awning that spanned the length of the entire motel. From the corner of my eye, I could see the fucker that shot at me from behind as he took off in a rusted white car from the 1950s. But before the bastard could get away, I quickly dug my pistol out of one of the pockets of my leather coat and fired at him, watching the bullet smash the glass and enter the side of his head. The dude was killed instantly, causing the car to swerve into the pickup truck. All of this happened in a matter of seconds as the door to Goldman's room opened and two men dressed in black came at me with guns blazing. Before any of their bullets could whiz in my direction, I jumped high into the air and drop-kicked him in the throat. The guy was dead before he hit the ground.

Seeing that the target he was trying to destroy just murdered his boy with a single kick to the throat, the second gunman became frozen with fear, paralyzing the motherfucker's trigger finger. Within that small window of cease fire, I grabbed the bastard's neck and snapped it like a twig. After the dude's body fell limply to the ground, I quickly made my way inside Goldman's motel room. Upon entering the room, my sense of smell was assaulted by the pungent scent of shit and vomit, a grotesque mixture that indicated that someone was being tortured before being disposed of. I feared the worst for Goldman. I could feel anxiety coursing through my veins as my eyes scanned the entire room, but to no avail.

Goldman was nowhere to be found. The room was in complete shambles. An end table that would have normally been beside the bed looked like it had been thrown across the room, smashed against the wall that faced the foot of the bed. A black leather-bound Bible was sticking out of its open drawer, grotesquely looking like a thick tongue, making the end table resemble the carcass of a dead animal. The mattress on the twin bed was bloodstained in various places. Some of the stains were fresh, while others began to brown and orange with time gone by.

The mattress itself was slightly askew on the bed, revealing part of the skeletal bed frame. Even the walls above had splotches of dried blood on them. Yup, Goldman had definitely put up a fight, but *where the fuck was he?* I had a gut feeling that he wasn't dead. For God's sake, I had spoken to him thirty minutes prior. I knew that was faulty logic, but I had to cling on to something. That's when it dawned on me to call his cell phone. To my surprise, I could hear the standard xylophone ringtone of Goldman's iPhone going off in the bathroom. I quickly bounded there, hope beginning to wash over me.

"Please God, let Don be alive," I caught myself reciting in a mantra as I opened the door. Letting Goldman's phone ring until its voicemail picked up, I reached into the darkened bathroom and flicked on the light before stepping in, revealing a hog-tied Goldman looking up at me from a mustard yellow bathtub with despair in his eyes.

Goldman began to squirm, begging me to untie him. His despair built up with every groan and mumble barricaded by the duct tape covering his mouth. With a mix of pity and relief washing over me, I removed the duct tape with one quick tug.

"Fuuuck! Dude, did you have to do that so hard?" whined Goldman. As I untied him, he began to talk nervously, in rapid succession, as though a pipe full of emotions had burst inside of him.

"Man, I thought I was a goner for sure. When those two Spanish guys came knocking at the door, I thought that it was you, so I opened it without checking who it was first. The next thing I know, those two bastards stormed in, tied me to the bed, and tortured me. They removed my toenails with pliers, and with a glowing hot straight razor, removed chunks of my flesh."

I don't know why Goldman was telling me all of this when I could clearly see what those bastards had done to him with my own eyes. I think he was talking because the sound of his own voice assured him that he was alive.

"Dude, I don't know what the fuck you did to get yourself into this mess, but you're gonna have to tell me everything," I said, now untying his hands and feet. "Do you think you can walk on your own?" I attempted to pull him up on his feet, but to no avail.

"Fuck it, I'll carry you," I said, swooping Goldman over my shoulder like a sack of potatoes and out of the motel room. Swinging the door open, I heard rapid footsteps approaching, which made me quickly take out my pistol and point it at the doorway. As the owner of the running footsteps appeared, I didn't even give him a chance to pass the threshold before I blasted him. With the dude's head lying in a pulpy heap of his brains, I realized that he must have been the proprietor of the motel. His shotgun lying forlornly beside his outstretched hands and his plaid shirt drenched in blood, it was obvious that the dude was only trying to defend his joint from the chaos happening. I shook my head in pity and stepped over the dude's body and crossed the graveled parking lot, which now resembled a warzone in Iraq.

When I made it to the van, I plopped Goldman in the passenger seat and went to the back of the van to search for one of those bombs. Finding one, I shut the back door to the van and approached Goldman's Benz, smashing the driver's side door in, and setting the bomb on the dashboard.

After setting up the bomb in Goldman's car, I made sure to grab all the shit in his glove compartment—license, registration, and anything that could lead back to Goldman being there. Shit, I even took the damn license plate off for good measure and hauled ass back to the van. As I hopped in the driver's seat, an earsplitting thunderclap shook the earth and the van, causing me to look through my rearview at the Benz and the motel office engulfed in flames. *Shit.* Thank God Goldman parked his car so close to the registration office. With any luck, the flames would consume the entire motel, leaving no evidence that we were ever there. Sirens started to wail in the distance with the moaning of death echoing throughout the atmosphere. Two miles away and counting, Goldman and I were already speeding down the highway.

CHAPTER TWELVE

"**Y**OU BETTER START TALKING, MOTHERFUCKER, I JUST risked my life for you," I said, letting my anger get the best of me. Goldman looked at me like a deer caught in the headlights, and then went on staring out the windshield in silence. I could feel the rage start to boil in the pit of my stomach, as if it were a cauldron bubbling over. Screeching to a halt on the side of the road, I pulled out my pistol and pointed the barrel underneath Goldman's jaw.

I growled, "Look motherfucker, you better tell me what of kind of shit you had going on with the Zepedas family before I finish the job those two faggots back there couldn't do."

With terror overshadowing his face like a storm cloud over the sun, Goldman began to speak in a heavy stutter. "I, um... was laundering m-money f- f-for Tony a-and decided t- t-to take a little off the top f- for m- m-myself." Goldman said this as if his vocal cords had trouble pushing sound out to make words.

Without giving it much thought, I took my pistol and whipped him across the face with it, splitting open his lips, instantly turning his mouth into a bloody maw. "You stupid fuck, what did you think you were in a fucking movie?!" I yelled in his face, trying to avoid looking at his pitiful mask of fear. "Jesus, you stupid fuck. You gave Tony information about me, didn't you?"

Suddenly, all the love I had for Goldman was swallowed by a tide of anger and hatred. He was in on Sheila's kidnapping. I could feel every fiber in my being holding me back from busting two shots in Goldman's dome. *"Don't do it, nigga. You need that piece of shit right now,"* admonished Carter's voice, cooling down my anger some. As if reading my mind, Goldman started to speak rapidly, as if trying to get everything off his chest at once.

"Look man, it wasn't my fault. They threatened me and the wellbeing of my family. One of those motherfuckers is even dating my mom down in Florida, so if I fuck up, they'll kill her. You gotta understand that I couldn't let that happen. I love my mom, man," Goldman whined like a frightened little boy. His eyes began welling up with tears as remorse started to bear its weight on his conscience, but the rage that bubbled showed no pity for him and drove me to pistol whip him again.

"When did Tony first approach you about laundering his money?" I asked calmly, as though we were two homies kicking it on the back porch and not two dudes caught in a life-and-death situation.

"The deal went down two months before you got out of prison," said Goldman in a matter-of-fact tone, despite blood pouring from his mouth. "Look man, after the laundering deal went down, Tony and his fucking goons came back to my office the next day and started asking mad questions about you. They wanted to know if you had family living in or around Delaware. They also wanted to know where you would be staying upon your release from prison. When I didn't divulge this information, that's when they threatened my family, showing me a picture of my mom out having dinner with her new boyfriend at a restaurant. Jesus, Sammy, understand that I had no fucking choice. I had to protect my family."

With Goldman's words digging into my soul like sharpened daggers, I raised my pistol, pressed it to his forehead, and asked through gritted teeth, "What about *my* family, motherfucker? You put Sheila in danger. You let them know my every move. You're lucky I need your ass right now, otherwise, I would've lit your ass up by now."

Goldman went cross-eyed as he looked at the barrel of the pistol pressed against his forehead.

"But you're lucky, you know why? Because as fucked up as it seems, you're the only one that I can trust right now."

Before responding, Goldman took a deep breath, as if swallowing a huge amount of fear. "What do you want me to do?" he asked, sounding like a little boy about to get hazed by a school bully.

I lowered the pistol from his forehead, hoping to alleviate some of the stress that I'd created for him so that he could talk and think more confidently. "I know that you're aware of motherfuckers that want to take down Tony as much as do. I also know that you act as an attorney for some of those cats."

Goldman's eyes began to light up as if the person that came to his mind suddenly flicked a switch in his brain.

"Of course, how could I forget him?" asked Goldman quietly, as if talking to himself. He looked up at me with a fresh glow of determination beaming from his face, as if the beating he suffered from Tony's goons never happened.

He cleared his throat. "In 2006, I defended this cat named Andre Austin, a veteran of the Iraq War. Serving in the military, he was given the nickname 'Pyro' for his expertise in explosives. Anyway, long story short, he was captured and tortured by an insurgence group, which left the poor bastard literally half-crazy. Fuck, he was so crazy that he murdered the entire rescue team that saved his ass. He even chopped some of those dudes into little pieces. Pyro was court marshaled for that shit, but I helped him escape the death penalty by copping an insanity plea. He spent five years in an asylum until his escape in 2011, when he found out that his wife and kids were murdered by the Zepedas family. So, if anyone has an axe to grind with Tony, it's Pyro."

Letting all that sink in, I couldn't stop the next question from coming out of my mouth, though I hated how desperate and hopeless I sounded. "Do you know where they're keeping Sheila, Don?"

He nodded with a grave look. "When those two assholes had me tied up in the bathroom of my motel room, I overheard them saying that Sheila was being held captive in a warehouse somewhere in Philadelphia, but they moved her to a compound down in Florida." The words came out of Goldman's mouth a mile a minute, as though he was afraid that he wouldn't get them out in time before I broke his jaw.

"Is there any chance that this Pyro dude can help me find her?" I asked, hoping against hope.

Goldman's face lit up like a Christmas tree. "There's only one way to find out." He grabbed his phone and began to tap wildly on the screen, sending Pyro a text message. "We're in!" he said gleefully after sending the text. "He wants to meet with us as soon as possible."

CHAPTER THIRTEEN

TWILIGHT WAS CREEPING ON THE EDGE OF THE HORIZON as we approached Pyro's hideout. According to Goldman, he was the one that helped Pyro go into hiding when he escaped the asylum, providing him with an apartment located below his rundown liquor store.

"Why are you helping this guy by putting yourself at risk," I asked, letting curiosity wash over me.

"I just felt sorry for the dude, sue me," Goldman shrugged, as if helping out escaped mental patients was an everyday occurrence for him. "Park right here, dude."

A dilapidated three-floored building came into view on the left side of the road. Its faded pink siding was peeling around the edges, revealing how rotted the structure was. A flashing blue and red OPEN sign blinked in its window, as if letting the world know that it was still alive and kicking.

With a squealing of its brakes, I parked the van on the curb and got out to assist Goldman out of the passenger seat. Careful not to touch any of Goldman's wounds, I set him down feet-first on the pavement, letting him gather his bearings.

"This way," Goldman said, directing me toward a narrow set of stairs that led down to Pyro's apartment, its door a faded whitewash that was peeling off and revealing splinters of aging wood. The scuffed window beside the door emanated a soft, warm glow, as loud hip-hop music vibrated through its pane.

"Well, at least we know that he's home," said Goldman with a slight nervous laugh.

Knocking at the door, Goldman began to tense up, as if he was an animal in the wild that could sense danger.

"Damn, dude! Will you calm the fuck down? I thought this Pyro cat was your man and shit. Your ass is acting like we about to meet the devil himself," I said, trying to hold back laughter that was about to bust out of my chest.

Goldman looked down at his feet, ashamed. "Sam, you don't know Pyro like I do. That man's a one-man army. He whipped out an entire platoon by himself."

I could see the fear flooding into Goldman's eyes. I had to stifle a laugh that crawled from the depths of my gut and desperately wanted to escape from the back of my throat. "You make this cat sound like a superhero or some shit," I said with a little bit of a giggle.

"Shit, laugh all you want, but Pyro was riddled with bullet holes when they found his ass wandering the streets of Baghdad. Shit, I'm talking some real Luke Cage shit. When they asked the motherfucker what he thought kept him alive, he told them revenge was the reason."

As Goldman was finishing up his story, the door to the apartment swung open, revealing a tall, husky Black man with thick black frames on his scarred face and a black-and-white Yankees cap. His crisp white tee hung loosely off his body as if he had lost a tremendous amount of weight. Looking at the dude's face, he was a dead ringer for K'wan, the urban crime novelist.

"Damn, nigga, what the fuck happened to you?" Pyro asked Goldman as we walked in.

"I had a little run-in with Zepedas's goons," Goldman said sheepishly.

"Shit, I'll say! It looks like you got hit by a fucking Mack truck then got attacked by a rabid wolf," said Pyro, examining Goldman from head to toe. "Dude, you better let me take a look at you real quick." His voice filled with fatherly concern, nothing at all like I expected a crazed soldier's voice to be.

Pyro took hold of Goldman and helped him walk to a beat-up blue armchair that had yellow stuffing protruding from its arms and sides. As Goldman sat down, he stripped down to his boxer shorts, revealing a heavy amount of bruising around his torso and also the two large gashes where the bastards took out chunks of flesh. Despite how bad he looked, Goldman's eyes emanated peace, as if he was finally at home. On the real, though, I thought that motherfucker was going to die in that damn armchair. Meanwhile, Pyro busied himself around the small apartment, gathering the essentials needed to tend to Goldman's wounds. I was kind of shocked at how that dude was to Goldman. Nowhere was there a trace of the war-torn monster that Goldman described minutes earlier. As a matter of fact, I even doubted that this dude could go up against Tony and his goons. That was, until my eyes swept the entire living room, if I could call it that.

To say that Pyro had had a living room was somewhat of a lie because the room that I was standing in at that moment was nothing short of a war room or science lab. All kinds of maps were posted high above battered steel work benches that ran the length of the walls on either side. On the maps themselves were pictures of high-ranking members of the Zepedas family, all of whom I knew personally. Hell, even my picture was posted on one of those maps, except where the word "Enforcer," was once written a huge line had been drawn through it. The words "Pyro's Ally" was written beside it. I could see right then and there that Pyro's vendetta with the Zepedas family ran deeper than mine. Shit, this dude knew where every member of the family rested their heads. This was indicated by the pinpoints he had tacked up on every street on the maps. Then the question hit me like a ton of bricks. If this dude knew where everybody rested their heads, why didn't he just snuff them out and get it over with?

"What's going on, B, you like my map?" Pyro's voice boomed from behind me, almost making me shit myself.

"My bad, man, I didn't mean to scare you," Pyro said sarcastically. His scarred face split into a grotesque smile that took up the entire bottom half, as if to say, "I know what you were thinking, nigga. I am going to kill all those fools, but you got exempt. This is your lucky day!" The awkwardness of the moment seemed to smother me, as I couldn't decide whether to trust the dude or not. I mean, I *was* on a list of men that were going to be killed by this man.

I cleared my throat, as if the mere sound of me removing phlegm from my throat shattered the wall of awkward silence and helped catapult my question. "I don't get it, if you know where all these fuckers rest their heads, why don't you light them all up and get it over with?"

Pyro roared with laughter, as if the sound of my question tickled him to the core of his soul. "Aww, man, you don't get it, do you? One doesn't kill for the sake of revenge. No, killing a motherfucker is an art form. It takes time. You see, every motherfucker on this planet is born to be a killer. It's in our DNA, you know. It's a natural tool that God gave man for our survival. We needed it to capture our prey. To sit back in the shadows and observe every minute detail of their actions until you catch your prey in their most vulnerable moment, then pounce on the fucker with full force."

Pyro finished his speech with a demon-like gleam in his eye, as if he was keeping something from me. He looked as if he had finally obtained what he wanted for so very long. On the real, the dude freaked me the fuck out.

Pyro cleared his throat and continued. "You see, once you discover your prey's vulnerability, you become an artist because now you came up with a way to subdue your prey and survive. Remember, survival is an art unto itself."

Pyro then grabbed a rectangular object that had a glossy screen the size of a hardback book. He turned it on and gave his full attention to the screen. "Oh, shit nigga, this you?!" Pyro said gleefully, turning the screen toward me. To my surprise, the screen displayed a black-and-white picture of me from the nineties, standing on the corner of Lancaster and Harrison with my hands in my pockets. Alongside the photo was the cover of my book, *Confessions of a Hitman*. The cover itself displayed a man's silhouette with his back against the wall, his gun cocked at his side as he stared out the window. *Sheila would have loved to see that,* I thought as my heart started to scream out in pain for the first time since the shit hit the fan the day before. My eyes started to well up with tears that I so desperately wanted to hold back but couldn't. I was swept away by the wild currents of my emotions, literally falling to my knees. I wept shamelessly in front of Pyro. The force of my sobs made my chest heave with a primal, guttural sound. Pyro stared at me impassively, as if watching a cold-blooded murderer who broke down into tears was an everyday occurrence for him.

After a few seconds, Pyro took a couple of steps toward me and helped me to my feet. "Holy fuck," he said mesmerized. "I've never seen such a beautiful demon in my life." I looked at him like he had lost his mind. Ashamed, I could feel my old homophobic feelings creeping into my heart.

As if reading my mind, Pyro said, "Not like that, nigga! What I mean is that you have love in your heart. If you were a *real* demon, you wouldn't have broken down into tears just now. Real demons don't have emotion. We entertain ourselves by subduing our prey and creating our art. But you, you are different. There is a great deal of love in your heart, I can feel that. Man, I can tell that being a killer is not in your blood, you were taught to be one. Or…maybe there was somebody who taught you how to be human. Whatever the case, I know what will help shed that demon flesh right off you. Peep this out real quick," said Pyro, walking toward an open doorway that had a blueish glow emanating from it.

As I followed Pyro into the room, I couldn't help but feel vulnerable and weak for letting him see me so exposed like that. According to Carter's teachings, me blubbering on the floor was the ultimate sign of my weakness, giving Pyro an opening to kill me. However, something deep down inside me suggested that I trust him.

I was greeted by a huge bank of closed-circuit TVs that took up an entire wall of the room.

"You see this shit right here, homie?" asked Pyro, gesturing toward the TVs proudly. "These are my eyes and ears to the Zepedas organization." He stretched out his arms wide as if showing off artwork. Below the bank of closed-circuit TVs was a strange panel that displayed what seemed like a million buttons. Shit, if I didn't know any better, I would have guessed that the room that I was standing in was some kind of situation room found at a government agency. Each TV screen displayed a different room in a giant facility that I wasn't familiar with.

As if already knowing that I didn't know what those TVs were monitoring, Pyro looked at me and said, "It looks to me that the Zepedas crew kept you in the dark about a lot of things." A dry smile cracked his face once again as if saying, *You poor ignorant fuck, you didn't know that you were just a worthless pawn.* Shaking his head as if to get rid of that thought, Pyro began, "What you're looking at right now is Tony's new drug facility that is located on a huge twenty-acre farm in Dover, Delaware." Shit, if I didn't know any better, I'd have sworn that Pyro sounded like a real estate agent trying to sell me a piece of property.

"On this farm, Tony is able to produce all the cocaine and heroin his heart desires, cutting out the main supplier. In other words, Tony doesn't have to worry about getting his product overseas. Nope, he is now his own supplier. That nigga is sitting pretty if you ask me." He pressed various buttons on the console to make one of the images on one of the TVs take up the entire bank.

"I know what you're thinking," Pyro stated, a huge smile on his face. "How the fuck can that nigga grow his own coke and heroin in a place like Delaware? This bum-fuck of a state doesn't have the climate for that shit." He taps a key on the console, changing the image on the TVs to one of a factory, which housed massive steel machines attached to at least three conveyor belts, chugging out package after package of cocaine and heroin.

"All of the shit you see there is synthetic. Not a single plant in nature had anything to do with it," said Pyro, his voice drenched in awe. "The thing is, I have no fucking idea what substances or materials Tony's using to fabricate the drugs.

"Another crazy thing about this entire operation is that the drugs made in this factory have the same effect on a junkie as the real thing. It's hard to tell the difference. I tried it out for myself," he said nonchalantly, as if describing the great taste of a vintage wine.

Before Pyro got back to the topic at hand, he took one quick glance my way and said, "Don't worry, nigga, I ain't no junkie." A booming baritone laugh escaped from deep down his chest, as if it was the sound of an enslaved soul finally set free, a total and complete contradiction of what Pyro's physical being represented. He cleared his throat and continued talking, gesturing toward the bank of closed-circuit TVs. "I know what you're thinking. How the fuck did this nigga install cameras on that highly guarded compound without anyone in the Zepedas crew catching wind of it? The answer to that question is simple. I had a nigga working for me on the inside, who you may know as Ace. That's right, your homie was a double agent, helping me get intel on Tony's entire organization. All I had to do was arm him with a flash-drive that he plugged into the facility's security camera's main computer terminal, and.... badda bing badda boom, I was in that ass like a thong, nigga." A huge smile cracked on Pyro's face as he marveled at his own genius. "Not only that, nigga, I could blow that entire facility to hell by just typing in a code on this console."

His words made my head spin. I couldn't believe that an enemy of the Zepedas family would have that much control over the fate of their organization. It was mind-boggling.

"Hold up, if you have the ability to destroy that facility why haven't you done it yet?" I asked, watching Pyro's grin spread wider, exposing his gums.

"I was waiting for a purpose that was greater than my own. You see, as a soldier, one goes into battle not for oneself, but for others. And today, I have finally found a greater purpose other than myself." He stopped talking and tapped on the console's keyboard. Suddenly, the image of the facility's factory was replaced by an image of Sheila in an empty room, lying on her side on a concrete floor with her nightie on. My soul began to struggle within the confines of my body, trying to grab her through the monitor only to fail and become a tear sliding down my face.

"Easy there, Beautiful Demon, we'll get her back," said Pyro, determination blazing in his eyes.

PART TWO:
PYRO

CHAPTER FOURTEEN

I couldn't help whistling John Phillip Sousa's "Stars and Stripes Forever" as I disposed of Sammy's white van and the two Latino niggas that were following it.

"Ha, fucking amateurs," I scoffed, glancing at my rearview mirror. There lay two corpses, whose necks bore the grotesque smile of Death that only I could bring. From what I observed through that mirror, I slit their throats so bad that their tendons looked as if they were having a bit of difficulty trying to keep their heads attached to their necks. They were tilted at grotesque angles that resembled an old jack-in-the-box spring worn out from age and tangled limply out of the left side of its box as if waiting for someone to put it back in.

"Top of the morning to ya, motherfuckers," I said in a mocking tone as I looked at the corpses through the rearview mirror. "It looks like y'all two need a bath in the Brandywine River." Starting up the engine, my mind quickly turned itself on autopilot, letting my mind roam free back to the memory of my two most recent kills. (Shit, Lord knows that I have done my fair share of "disposing" to know what route led to the Brandywine River, so, I was straight.)

Letting my mind rewind itself like an old VHS tape, I went back to two hours prior, where I had left Sammy in a pitiful heap of despair in front of a huge screen displaying the love of his life lying unconscious in her nightie on the concrete floor of a cell. Shit, I'm not going to front, watching Sammy touch that screen as if his hand had the power to transcend it and touch his beloved's cheek tugged at my heartstrings (or, what was left of them anyway). Shit, truth was, Sammy reminded me of Emanuel. He was my first and only true love, which was why I felt an overwhelming sense to protect and help Sammy get his girl back if it's the last thing I did. On the real, it was because I felt this overwhelming sense in helping Sammy on his mission that I could sense Zepedas's goons a mile away. Taking my eyes away from the pitiful heap of Sammy lying on the floor in front of the monitor, I made my way toward the exit of my apartment, the basement of an old liquor store converted into a living space. It was littered with photos of all my enemies and maps of their homes, places of businesses, and much more.

"How you holding up, Goldman?" I asked the man who slouched on the pea-green recliner in the middle of the room, without taking my attention away from the rectangular gap that I use as a peephole to the steel door to see what's on the other side. So far, all that I could see was the darkness of night open like the mouth of an endless chasm, but the soldier's instinct encompassing my body at the moment was gearing me up for a battle.

"Dawg, I'm just trying to hang in there," said Goldman, with fatigue outlining his voice.

I turned away from the door to get a better look at him, hoping against hope that glance will somehow rejuvenate the man that sat in a pale, broken down heap of stab wounds and a bloodied undershirt, a shell of his former self. No longer did Goldman represent the self-assured young lawyer that he once was. His eyes no longer shone with the intensity and pride of a man that seemed to have the law in his pocket. No, that was drained out of him when Tony Zepedas's men tortured him in that New Jersey motel room. In other words, the dude that I was looking at now was nothing less than a zombie version of himself, a dead man walking. The paleness that shrouded his being was an indicator that Goldman wasn't long for this world.

"How's our boy holding up?" asked Goldman, nodding toward my war room, where Sammy Ortega kneeled in front a bank of CRT monitors showing his love lying unconscious on a cold concrete floor. Pity surged through my body. With his gaze transfixed on the monitors, it was clear to me that at this very moment, Sammy's soul had left his body and was trying to transcend space and time to be with his beloved.

"Man, that's pitiful," said Goldman shaking his head shamefully. "To think that emotional wreck back there was once consider one of the most feared hitmen on the face of the earth." He snorted with disgust, as his mind traveled to a much stronger and powerful image of Sammy.

Yeah, well, pussy will do that to a man sometimes," I said with a sigh, turning my attention back to the front door. My soul was becoming anxious and preparing for any second. As if on cue, a beam of headlights glared past the peephole, catching my attention. *You stupid fucks. When you go to kill someone, you make sure that you cut off the damn headlights before you arrive on the scene.* This thought bounced around the chambers of my mind, causing its loud echo to awaken my darkness.

"It's showtime, baby," I whispered to myself. The darkness inside began to climb from the pit of my stomach to the center of my heart, as if it was an anxious child in a rush to get home from school to play their new videogame console. Once the darkness settled comfortably deep within the cackles of my heart, I transformed into Death itself, ready to destroy anything in my path.

Without giving it a second thought, I opened the door and quickly took cover against the cement wall of the staircase leading down to my basement apartment. Feeling the cool wall against my back, I let myself become reacquainted with the shadows that had protected me my entire life, my eternal armor.

"You sure this is where that nigga's hiding?" The question drenched in a Spanish accent floated to my ears from the black Honda Accord parked in the graveled parking lot. The windows from the driver's side door lowered completely, revealing the dude that I would soon kill.

"Weren't you paying attention, motherfucker? We've got surveillance on this faggot for days!"

"Jesus Christ, man. You need to calm the hell down. I was just asking a question."

From the sound of their bickering, it was easy to see that the two men did not have their attention on their mission, giving me ample time to sneak in the back seat of their car. Utilizing the sound of their bickering to shroud my movements on the parking lot gravel, I crouched and crept toward one of the back doors of the Accord. Luckily, the door that I chose to enter from had its window partially down, allowing me to stick my hand down the opening and pop the lock up with my thumb and forefinger, thanking my lucky stars the car didn't have power locks. Quietly opening the door and making my way into the backseat, I swiftly removed the knife that I had concealed up my sleeve, and with rapid movement, slit the throats of both men before they knew what hit them.

"Such fucking amateurs," I said, releasing a little snort of disgust at how incompetent those two were. Before I made my way out of the car, I sat back in the middle of the seat to admire my handiwork. The blood spatter on the windshield was rather elegant to me. The knife penetrated the fleshy part of their necks, cutting both men in one swift and precise motion. Now, as I sat relaxed in the backseat, I observed how two thick splatters of blood converged to form a crude rainbow-like arc on the windshield. *Oh, how gorgeous is that,* I thought. The two blood splatters have merged into one. Overcome by an emotion surging throughout my body, I couldn't help but notice the beauty on that windshield. The two splatters of blood connecting as one. *A marriage in death,* I thought, letting tears fall freely.

"Damn, I gotta stop being so fucking sensitive," I said aloud, as my heart gripped to the last bit of that memory while the present was rapidly approaching. That final piece of memory was of me leaning forward in the backseat to touch the blood on the windshield. As the fingertips of my right hand touched the blood, I swear I could feel both of those men's souls swimming around in it, almost making all the joy and pain that they once held in the world palpable. In essence, by simply touching that blood smear, they became a part of me. I now owned them. Their souls were food for the grotesque monster that was my soul. Yes, art at its finest. That was my final thought as I threw the two corpses into the river.

"Bye, bye my lovelies, you have served your purpose in my mission," I said in a dainty high-pitched voice, giving an effeminate wave to the corpses as they lazily rolled down the river.

CHAPTER FIFTEEN

T HE DAY BEGAN TO OPEN ITS EYES AS I DROVE TO A junkyard to dispose of Sammy's white van. Feeling the warm summer rays of the new day bathe my being, my thoughts turned back to Emanuel. A pang of longing overcame my heart and mind, bringing with it an overflow of memories that swept me away in its current. I once again turned my body on autopilot and let the wave take me where it willed.

Suddenly I saw the face of my beloved. His lips, full and plump, were always upturned in a slight smile, as if he was enjoying a private joke, he came up with himself. His eyes would dance every time he told a story or said something philosophical that would catch my heart and make me melt. Emanuel was unlike any other individual that I had ever met in my life, a complete oxymoron. Although highly intelligent, he was confined to a wheelchair. That isn't to say that people confined to wheelchairs aren't intelligent, but Emanuel would often say this his mind felt prisoner to his body, blinding people to who he was. Noticing that I wasn't understanding what he was saying, he cleared his throat and said, "When you first met me in our project lobby, what did you think of me?"

The answer to his question came quickly to my mind, however, I held myself back because I knew that my response might sting.

"I'll tell what you had thought of me that day," he said knowingly. "You more than likely felt sorry for me. Shit, maybe you were a little afraid to come near me, for fear that my disability was contagious. Or perhaps you thought that I was retarded."

"Nah, I wasn't thinking that at all," I lied. "When I first saw you, I was thinking about how fly your electric wheelchair looked. On the real, I was kind of envious of your getting to drive in a life-size Tyco RC."

"You lying asshole," Emanuel said, stifling a giggle. You know damn well that you thought I was retarded. It's okay to admit that you felt that way, dude. Everyone thinks that about disabled people at least one time in their lives. That is, until they get to know us on a more personal level."

In all honesty, Emanuel was right. I did stereotype him when I first saw him racing out of our lobby. He was chasing after a female crackhead that was so skinny she resembled a corpse whose body had long been picked clean by the maggots in its grave, except that corpse had been reanimated and was running full speed toward the exit with Emanuel's neon red backpack in hand.

I was pulled out of my reflection when Emanuel screamed, "Come back here with my shit, bitch!" Thick with rage, his voice bounced off the acoustics of the lobby. Witnessing this, I ran toward the woman and tackled her inches away from the exit.

Get off me, motherfucker!" screamed the woman. Her cries were both guttural and shrill at once, like a wounded animal that got its paw caught in a bear trap. Turning her on her back, I swung my right fist and connected with her jaw, causing a grotesque shatter to be the new sound to bounce off the lobby's acoustics. Snatching the backpack from her limp hand,

I turned my gaze toward the wheezing sound of the electric wheelchair coming straight at me, now inches from my face.

"Hey, thanks, man," he said to me, snatching his backpack in a brisk motion while trying to wipe the drool dripping down his chin. Honest to God, Emanuel scared the hell out of me at that moment. I thought he had contacted rabies. Failing to hide my fear from him, I quickly pulled my hand back for fear that he might bite it.

Noticing my fear, Emanuel said, "Dude, you don't have to be afraid of me. I promise that I won't bite you. If it's the drool that frightens you, I can assure you that nothing is wrong with me. Unfortunately, this ghastly drooling is a side effect of my cerebral palsy. I know that I look crazy and retarded, but I can't help it," he said, lowering his eyes in shame.

It was then that Emanuel's gaze landed in the grotesque burn scars that riddled my arm, resembling that of a geriatric man's.

"What happened to your arm, dude?" Emanuel's question began to open a scar of a memory, causing it to bleed out visions of my father making me put my entire right arm on the stove. It wasn't enough for him to just put my hand. Shaking my head as if to dislodge the memory from my mind, I turned my attention back to the crackhead pinned under me. The woman's jaw was visibly broken, its lower half resembled that of an old wooden dummy that lay abandoned in its owner's magic trunk for years.

"Let me go, motherfucker," the crackhead woman said weakly through her slacked jaw. Pity for her started to fill my heart. Letting my emotions get the best of me, I lessened my weight on her, allowing the woman to slip out from me as I stood up. Without a word, she quickly got to her feet and ran out of the lobby as if demons were chasing her out of hell. A smile creased my features as I watch the woman run north toward Market Street.

Turning to face Emanuel, I finally caught a full glimpse of his features. His hair was slicked back with gel, reminding me of a 1950s greaser. His eyes sparkled with a vibrant light that radiated throughout his entire being. It was like his soul was coming out to greet me, letting me partake in its beauty. His mouth was outlined with beautiful plump lips, the color of salmon, just begging to be kissed. I couldn't take it much longer. I needed to touch him so that I could obtain some of his beauty, but I didn't want to come off weird or offensive. To my surprise, however, Emanuel grabbed my scarred arm and kissed it, leaving his lips pressed upon it for a full twenty seconds with his eyes closed.

When releasing my arm, he opened his eyes and said, "I can feel your pain. Please share it with me. If you ever want to talk or anything, I'm in Apartment 1A. I'm always home if you need me." With that, he backed up his wheelchair and sped out of the exit into the morning sun, leaving me with tears running down my face. It was right then and there that I fell in love with Emanuel and wanted desperately to bask in the aura of his beauty. It was as if my soul was climbing out of my eyes and down my cheeks to grab some of his beauty and abscond with it.

Following the week after the incident in our project lobby, I took Emanuel up on his offer and visited his apartment. It was as though my soul was attracted to the light that radiated behind that door. I was a moth to a flame. To put it mildly, my visits to Emanuel's were nourishment to my soul, allowing my emaciated soul to gorge on the feast that was his love and intelligence. For it was during such visits that he would school me on the great philosophers, while eating rice and beans or *arroz con pollo.* (I loved Puerto Rican food.) Emanuel once explained to me that a psychologist named Viktor Frankel stated that to live was to suffer, and to survive meant that we must discover the meaning in our suffering. Touched by the profound meaning of those words, tears of shame fell freely from my eyes as I confessed to him that Otis, my stepfather, would come into my room at night and rape me, forcing his old smelly dick to rip through my asshole, making it bleed the first time he attacked me. Not only did he repeatedly rape me, but he would also lock me up in a kettle cage whenever I disobeyed him, forcing me to eat my excrement. With tears stinging my eyes, I also confessed to Emanuel that I had slit my stepfather's throat as he slept on the living room couch. Disposing of Otis's body was a breeze. Owing to my Uncle George's job at Delaware Waste Management as a garbage collector—he also hated Otis with passion for beating my mom to death and throwing her down a flight of stairs—he helped me wrap the body in a huge garbage bag, tossing it in a dumpster so that the garbage truck he worked on could pick it up the next morning.

"Man, that's some serious shit," said Emanuel, his eyes as big as saucers. I could feel the mixture of horror and amazement conjure grotesque murder scenes in his mind, making me smile.

"Don't sweat it, nigga, I ain't no crazed maniac. I just had to do what I had to do," I said casually, as if I just told him that I had returned from the grocery store a few minutes ago.

"Just so you know, your secret is safe with me," said Emanuel in a low, paternal tone. His words washed over me like warm soapy water. I can honestly admit that at that very moment I felt the safest I had ever been in my entire life. So safe, in fact, that I let myself be driven by impulse and emotion. I kissed Emanuel passionately. It was on that day that we declared our love for one another.

CHAPTER SIXTEEN

THE MEMORY OF OUR FIRST KISS BEGAN TO DISSOLVE into the present day. No longer was I in Emanuel's apartment sharing a kiss, but out on the open road driving a van to a junkyard to be destroyed. I could feel my heart start to capsize with the weight of the emotion it carried in a sea of anger, now forming a tidal wave that consumed me with rage.

"Goddamn you, Sammy! You were the one who took my love away from me. You were the motherfucker who murdered Emanuel in cold blood."

I said all of this out loud as images of Sammy shooting Emanuel in the chest flashed before my mind's eyes. I swerved the van over to the side of the road before I lost control. Punching the steering wheel with all my might, I managed to break the van's horn. This triggered an everlasting wail of pain, as if someone were resting their hand on it for an eternity.

Tears streaming down my eyes, I noticed that the van had run out of gas. I hopped out of the van and stood in the middle of the road as a red sedan Ford approached. Noticing this, I quickly pulled my 9mm pistol from my waistband and waited as the car came to a screeching halt in front of me. I pointed my pistol directly at the young woman driving the car.

Frozen in fear, the young woman didn't get out of the car until I went over to the driver's side door, snatching her by her silky blond hair and pulling her entire petite frame out of the driver's side window. Before letting out a scream for help, I snapped her neck, throwing her lifeless body to the asphalt, not without noticing how stunning she looked in her black leggings and dark green crop top.

"Such a cute little White chick," I said to myself as I opened the door and got behind the wheel of the Ford, thankful that the road was practically deserted. Abandoning my original plan of destroying the van, I turned the car around and headed back home, ready to finish this once and for all.

CHAPTER SEVENTEEN

"WHAT'S GOOD, MAN?" SAID THE MALE VOICE ON THE other end of the phone line after five rings.

"Nigga, what took you so long to pick up your damn phone?!" I said angrily, letting my street language slip out.

"Shit, you sound just like my main ho when I don't answer her calls right away."

"Look motherfucker, this is some serious shit I have planned out, and it's all coming together. I don't need shit heads like you fucking it up," I said, scolding my henchman like an unruly child.

"Yo, you better shut down all that noise, dude," the man on the other end of the phone said, anger rising in his voice. "Just so your ass knows, I had to subdue your little friend. He tried to leave the apartment, so I shot him."

"You did what?!" I yelled, swerving the red sedan into the opposite lane, almost crashing head on with a Greyhound bus. "Nigga, tell me you didn't kill the bastard, please?" My voice was now drenched in a pleading shrill.

"Pyro, you need to relax, man. I just blew out both of his kneecaps with my trusty double barrel shotgun." The man on the other side of the phone became engulfed in bubbles of laughter. "I didn't kill the dude, alright? As soon as I saw him fall on his back, I picked him up and tied him up in the basement where the girl's at, just like you told me to. There's a problem, though. Your boy Goldman is dead. Yeah, the nigga must have bled out or something. I found him tore the fuck up in that ugly ass green chair you got in your living room."

"Oh well, the man served his purpose," I said nonchalantly. Goldman was just a pawn in my game. I had no further use for him whatsoever.

The same could be said for the man on the other end of the phone who had followed me around since the war with Iraq. His name was Jamal Mahammad, an African American Muslim on my platoon who was disgruntled with how Muslims were treated in America. The poor bastard let himself be brainwashed by me, believing I was going to start some sort of militia in the name of Allah. Little did he know, however, that once I ended the call abruptly without his knowledge, his cell phone would explode, dislodging shrapnel in his brain. *A rather ingenious explosive that I invented,* I thought, hanging up my cell without saying goodbye. My mind raced with future images of Jamal holding his ears as his eyes rolled back into his head while foaming at the mouth. It was kind of sad to think that the only body the authorities would find intact after this would be Jamal's.

CHAPTER EIGHTEEN

Arriving at my place, I could hardly contain my excitement. My palms were sweaty. I could feel my heart bang wildly against my rib cage, causing me to lose focus and talk to myself.

"Oh my God, *oh my God!* You will be avenged today, Emanuel. I will be by your side soon, baby!" I cheered in a singsong voice.

Opening the front door to the apartment, I was greeted to the grotesque image of Goldman's corpse lying slumped over in the easy chair as if he was sleeping, the wounds of his injuries open and gaping like the mouths of screaming banshees. The bloodstains on his shirt, once a shade of crimson, were now brown with a day of age. Forgetting about the horrific tableau before me, I made my way to the small kitchen in the back of my apartment where there was a manhole-like cover hiding a tunnel that I had been digging for about a year now, day and night, hoping that it wouldn't cave in on me.

Making my way down the rope ladder, I could feel Emanuel's presence all around me, comforting and giving me power beyond belief. Reaching the bottom, my feet touched the linoleum floor along with white brick walls. The whiteness was so bright that it hurt my eyes. Truth be told, if I hadn't built that dungeon myself, I would have sworn that I was on the set of the first *Saw* movie.

Chained up to the wall in front of me were an unconscious Sammy and Sheila, both of their heads dangling on their necks as if overtaken by sleep. Before walking any closer to my victims, I took the time to observe Jamal's handiwork. Both of the arms and legs of my victims were tied firmly, reminding me of Christ on the cross.

"Perfect," I muttered, stepping closer to Sammy, smacking him awake. Seeing the dazed and confused look on his face brought so much joy to me, I couldn't help but let out a little giggle.

"Wake up, beautiful demon," I said, watching Sammy shake the grogginess away.

His bleary eyes took in the room, and he calmly asked, "What the fuck, Pyro?" I had to laugh at his calm tone.

"Do you know why you're here?" I asked with a broad smile, but in place of an answer I received a scream as he suddenly noticed Sheila right beside him.

"Oh God, *please* don't hurt her," Sammy pleaded.

"It's funny you should say that. I felt the same exact way when you killed Emanuel. Did you have mercy on him? It wasn't his fault that his dad owed drug money to Zepedas, but you killed him anyway as a message to his father. Well, guess what? Emanuel's father didn't give a rat's ass about his son. That just gives him more time to hide. Did you ever catch the bastard by the way? No, you did not, but I did. He was holed up in a whore house in old San Juan. Yeah, I sliced his throat from ear to ear and stabbed to death the chick he was fucking. I know what you're asking yourself right now. 'What was so important about a crippled teenager,' right?

"Well, he was my lover. He taught me how to be human. He taught me I have self-worth. Hell, Emanuel even taught me how to speak proper English. The kid would often tell me that the worst part of living in the ghetto was that ignorance is often championed over intelligence. I swear, it was like Emanuel had a force field that would protect him from the ghetto. That is, until you killed him," I said, my voice cracking. "I was there hiding behind the couch, like a coward. It took me twenty-two years to set this moment up, but I did it. I was the one who pulled the strings to get you out of jail. I used Goldman to buy off the judge on your case. By the way, while you were in the joint, I wiped out Zepedas's entire crew, establishing me as the head of Delaware's drug trade."

I stopped talking, catching my breath as I dug my phone out of my back pocket. "To show you it is not all ill will toward you, I will read an excerpt from a review of your book." I cleared my throat and began to read from my phone.

"Not since *Fifty Shades of Grey* has a book made such an impact on its readers. Never before has a street biography touched the heart of so many with its poetic prose…" It was at that moment that I could feel the anger boil up in my chest and stopped reading, taking out my pistol and shooting both Sammy and Sheila in the chest. Giggling like a mad man, I got down on my knees and yelled, "Emanuel, you are avenged, my love!"

Putting the pistol to my temple, I pulled the trigger and let darkness consume me.

ABOUT THE AUTHOR

Juan Carlos Diaz received a Bachelor's of Psychology from Wilmington University. After four years of study, Diaz decided to write a crime fiction novel titled *Westside Wilmington Chronicles,* which is currently available via Amazon. Diaz currently resides in New Castle, Delaware where he writes poetry and crime fiction.

ALSO BY JUAN CARLOS DIAZ

Little Bites of Blue

Made in the USA
Columbia, SC
03 October 2024